The Evelyn R. Flug
Children's Library
PITKIN COUNTY LIBRARY
1 13 0002880556
PITKIN COUNTY LIBRARY
J FICTION J717ge JONES
Jones, Kimberly, 1957-
The genie scheme
15.99
WITHDRAWN
120 NORTH MILL ST. • ASPEN, CO 81611 • (970) 429-1900

D0016573

the Genie Scheme

Also by Kimberly K. Jones

Sand Dollar Summer

Margaret K. McElderry Books

the Genie Scheme

Kimberly K. Jones

Margaret K. McElderry Books
New York London Toronto Sydney

Margaret K. McElderry Books
An imprint of Simon & Schuster Children's Publishing Division
1230 Avenue of the Americas, New York, New York 10020

Book design by Krista Vossen
The text for this book is set in Manticore.
Manufactured in the United States of America
2 4 6 8 10 9 7 5 3
Library of Congress Cataloging-in-Publication Data
Jones, Kimberly, 1957–
The genie scheme / Kimberly K. Jones.
p. cm.
Summary: When twelve-year-old Janna, who lives in a small house with her single mother, helps a homeless woman who turns out to be a genie, she discovers how interconnected the world really is.
ISBN: 978-1-4169-5554-2
[1. Wishes—Fiction. 2. Genies—Fiction. 3. Conduct of life—Fiction.]
I. Title.
PZ7.J720455Ge 2009
[Fic]—dc22
2008020245

For my mother and father,
LaVonne Egemo Jones & Clyde Jones

*

Tusen takk
A thousand thanks

Acknowledgments

This book wouldn't be what it is without the
unerring eyes and sensibilities of Karen Wojtyla
and Sarah Payne, or the tenacious
efforts of agent Bill Reiss.

the
Genie
Scheme

Chapter 1

"Match all six numbers and be the winner of the Mega Multimillion Dollar Lotto Lottery!" brayed the skinny man on the TV. "This week's jackpot is three and a half million dollars!"

The camera swept to a tall blonde woman with freakishly long silver fingernails who was poised to pluck a numbered Ping-Pong ball as it popped out of the lottery bin.

Janna tightly gripped the pink slip of paper that could change her life. All week she had worried: What if she lost it? What if it got ripped? What if it was the winning ticket but it got wet and the precious magic numbers disappeared in a smear of ink, and her chance at happiness along with them? Or worst of all, what if her mom found the forbidden lottery slip and took it away—like last time?

"But we need the money, Mom!" Janna had moaned.

"The last thing that people who need money can afford is a lottery ticket!" Janna's mom had said.

"But if you don't buy a ticket, how can you ever win? You know, buy a ticket, buy a dream?"

"You have a greater chance of being struck by lightning, dear, yet I don't see you paying for a chance at that."

Then Janna's mother had held up the piece of paper that contained Janna's hopes, and had ripped it into very tiny, very unhopeful pieces and had flushed them down the toilet. It wasn't fair!

But that was last week; this was now. Janna had kept the lottery ticket in an envelope under her pillow ever since she'd bought it, and now the paper was safe in her hand, the numbers crisp and clear. It was the winning ticket, she simply knew it. Those six numbers would take that anxious look from her mother's eyes. Those magic integers would buy them a new car to replace their old and decrepit hatchback named Maybe, because maybe it would start and, then again, maybe it wouldn't. Those nice numerals would buy Janna anything and everything that she had ever, ever wanted or would ever, ever want. She would be just like Elizabeth Newby across the street—a modern day princess with the newest gadgets and gizmos, the neatest clothes, the coolest of everything cool. How happy those numbers would make her!

The first ball popped out, and the silver talons pounced.

"Check your tickets, Ladies and Gentlemen. The first number is . . . sixty-three!"

Janna didn't need to check her slip. She knew that sixty-three was on it.

The second ball hopped out.

"Thirteen! Lucky thirteen for some folks out there. Are you one of them?"

Yes, Janna was one of them.

The third ball appeared.

"The third number is nine. Three more to go! Are you still with us?"

Janna was. There was a slight pause before the fourth ball appeared, and for a moment Janna lost her hope, her resolve, her absolute belief that she held in her hand the ticket to more than three million dollars. The ball finally appeared.

"Fourth on our numbers hit parade today is twenty-two. Those of you who have matched four numbers are already winners! One hundred dollars to anyone who matches four out of six!"

Janna had already won one hundred dollars. She kissed the piece of paper, breathing sweet, supportive words into it.

"Thirty-one! Do you have a thirty-one?"

Janna didn't have to look. She had looked so many times that she knew the numbers on the pink slip by heart, but she looked all the same, just to make sure that the thirty-one hadn't disappeared.

It hadn't.

Five numbers out of six meant she had already won one thousand dollars, but if she didn't win the entire jackpot, she didn't want any money at all. They could keep their piddly thousand bucks!

The model's silver pincers snatched the final ball like a bird grabbing a worm. There was a horrible second as she fumbled the ball slightly instead of rotating it gracefully, and the painted number got lost in her palm.

"You klutz!" Janna shrieked at the TV. Then, afraid her bad temper would break the magic, she concentrated on being calm and serene.

Sixty-six, she breathed.

Sixty-six, she willed.

Sixty-six. She would do anything for a sixty-six.

Sixty-six. It had to be a sixty-six.

It wouldn't be fair if it was anything except sixty-six! Maybe if she said "sixty-six" sixty-six times?

Sixty-six. Sixty-six. Sixty-six. Sixty-six. Sixty-six. Sixty-six. . . .

The model had regained control of the ball and was slowly rotating it to the screen. There it was! It was . . . ninety-nine. Janna went cold and still. She felt as if she had just run full speed into a wall. She had been so close. Good-bye, new car. Hello, Maybe. It wasn't fair!

But wait—the silver talons were turning the ball. Here it came, right side up! The ninety-nine turned into a sixty-six! Sixty-six! Janna had known all the time that it had been a winning ticket! How could she ever have doubted it?

The man with the donkey voice was speaking. "We hope *you* were the lucky one, but if not, there's always *next* week's Mega Multimillion Dollar Lotto Lottery. Buy a dream for a dollar! Good night, folks!"

Janna stood in the center of the room, clutching the ticket to her chest. Now that she was rich, the very air she breathed seemed different. Now that she was rich, she would change a lot of things. Now that she was rich, she could have everything that Elizabeth Newby had. No, she could have *more* than Elizabeth Newby had, and *before* Elizabeth Newby had it.

Janna heard the door open behind her and turned to see her mom with an armful of groceries and a handful of mail. Janna jumped up and ran to her, knocking the mail into the air. She whooped and threw her arms around her mother. She heard glass break as the grocery bag fell to the floor, but Janna didn't care.

"I won! I won!"

Mom held Janna's shoulders and stared at her daughter. Janna waved the pink slip in her mother's face.

"We're rich! I won the lottery just like I always said I would!"

Janna's mom said nothing, but Janna could see the tiredness fall from her eyes, and she saw quite clearly the images that appeared in her mother's mind—a reliable furnace, a dishwasher, a new winter coat instead of a used one.

The telephone rang. Janna fell silent as her mother reached, dreamlike, for the phone.

"Hello?"

Janna could see her mother's hand tremble as she handed the receiver to Janna.

"Hello, Janna? This is the president of the United States. I just want to congratulate you on winning the lottery. It couldn't have happened to a nicer person!"

Janna nodded dumbly into the receiver.

"Say thank you," her mother hissed.

"Thank you," Janna squeaked.

When the president hung up, she handed her mother first the telephone and then the telephone book.

"Call up the car dealer. Tell them to bring over that new car we were looking at last week, the fancy convertible. Any color you want!"

It seemed that Janna had no sooner turned around to look out the window than a wrecker was hooking up Maybe to haul it away once and for all. The sleek, shiny blue sports car she and her mother had oohed and aahed over was pulling into Maybe's old place.

As her mother ran out to the car, Janna pulled the stack of catalogs from under her bed, the ones she liked to leaf through and checkmark the things she liked.

She dug her mother's credit card out of her purse on the kitchen table and picked up the phone. To save time Janna just ordered one of everything in the first catalog and requested express delivery. Immediately, the doorbell rang. All the things she had ordered had arrived! She had everything stacked in the hall while she dialed the phone number of the next mail-order company.

"Janna," her mother called. "Janna!"

Janna looked out the window to see her mother standing by their new car with a fur coat on over an expensive-looking red dress. Shiny jewels sparkled from her ears, her neck, her wrist.

Janna waved, yet her mother still shouted, "Janna! Janna!"

"Yeah, Mom, I see you. Cool!"

"Janna!"

Janna opened her eyes carefully. Her mother was standing in the bedroom doorway.

"What's cool, Janna?"

"Nothing," Janna said.

"Hurry up, lazybones. We need to get a move on if you want to get the best pick of winter coats. I'll go try to start Maybe. Don't forget to bring your money for the bookstore."

Janna turned her head to look out the window. Maybe stood in the driveway like a diseased and disgusting bug. She felt under her pillow. There it was, her pink lottery ticket from last night's lottery. She remembered now. She hadn't even matched one number in the Mega Multimillion Dollar Lotto Lottery.

Reality stunk.

Chapter 2

"I don't get it," her mother said on the way to the thrift store. "Your friends run around looking like ragbags, but the rags need to be new and only certain brands."

Janna was still grouchy from the bursting of her dream bubble, so she retreated to that convenient, overused phrase.

"You don't understand."

Her mother was silent for a moment, and Janna wondered fleetingly if she had been a little snappish. She knew that her mother had been dealing with a lot of nasty stuff lately as chair of the middle school board. This year's budget had failed to pass twice, and Carol Danner had been spending a lot of hours at some very wretched meetings.

Janna was about to apologize when her mother spoke quietly.

"I do understand, Janna, but I also understand that we

only have so much money to feed us, clothe us, and pay the bills. This is what we have to do right now."

Twenty minutes later Janna was in the store, trying to look invisible, which wasn't too difficult because there were a lot of people engrossed in hunting for bargains. She was pretty sure none of her schoolmates would come in here, but you never knew who knew somebody else, and she wouldn't be able to stand it if word got out that she bought most of her clothes secondhand. It wasn't her fault she was growing so fast that she needed a second winter coat this season. She sighed. It wasn't her mom's fault either, and the old coat *was* so tight it didn't keep her warm. If there was one thing Janna hated, it was being cold. She hated everything about it, from how it made her nose run and the way the frozen runoff chapped her upper lip, all the way down to how her toes felt (before they got numb and she could no longer feel them, that is) as they pushed frigid and bloodless into the hard toe of her boots.

To Janna's embarrassment, her mother was right in the middle of the commotion. Unlike Janna, her mother was not put off by the less than attractive appearance of some of her fellow shoppers. She was carrying on a pleasant conversation with some woman who was missing a few teeth, while they each quickly and efficiently sorted through hats and mittens, holding them to the light to reveal hidden holes or frayed spots. The coat they had already agreed upon for Janna was draped over Carol's arm. It was not at all what Janna would have chosen, and it was a little too big (*then you can wear it next year too*), but Janna's mom had been so pleased by the label and condition of the coat (*it's such a good coat, Janna*) that Janna hadn't had the heart to argue. It usually went this way.

Janna was waiting as patiently as possible. When they were through at the thrift store, her mom was going to drive her to the bookstore. She had saved up enough allowance to buy *The Secret Princess*, the new installment in the Medieval Maids series. She had wanted to read it ever since it had come out, and the waiting list at the library was sooooo long. The Medieval Maids were three girls who disguised themselves as knights and went about the countryside doing good deeds of generosity and courage. They were always getting into dangerous predicaments, but they were smart and strong and expert in all the knightly skills, so they always got out of the predicaments as well. Janna liked to imagine herself as one of them. She was looking forward to spending her entire afternoon reading that book curled up with a cup of hot chocolate and maybe some of those flower-shaped chocolate striped cookies that she was so fond of.

Janna was sinking herself back into a rack of coats when she heard snarly voices arguing. She looked up to see a woman not much taller than herself addressing the cashier, waggling her cane at him. The woman's purple coat had one ripped elbow, and its hem nearly dragged on the ground. Below her coat the toes of men's black galoshes peeked out. Beside her was a purple vinyl shopping bag that had been carefully patched with gray duct tape in spots. Each handle was wrapped thoroughly with tape as well. Janna could see a tube of toothpaste, a pair of thick gray socks rolled into a ball, and the tatter of what looked like a blanket peeking out of the bag, as well as some returnable bottles. Janna knew about homeless people who carried all their earthly possessions with them. She and her friends called them bag people, although not when Janna's mother could hear. Janna tried to imagine putting all her possessions in one bag. Her stuffed animals alone wouldn't even begin to fit.

The bag lady was clutching a purple hat and several bills in the hand that wasn't holding the cane. The cashier was shaking his head, but the woman still pushed the hat and the money closer to him. Interested, Janna moved out of the coat rack and toward the checkout counter.

"Why not?" she heard the woman's raspy voice say, but Janna couldn't see her face.

"I told you, you don't have enough money," the cashier said, but he wasn't really paying attention to her anymore; his back was half-turned and he was already starting to help another customer.

"It's got a hole in it!"

"That's reflected in the price already. I'm sorry. You don't have enough money."

"But I need a warm hat. It was way below freezing last night, and it's supposed to be even colder tonight. My ears nearly fell off!"

"Buy a different hat. You don't have enough money for that one." The cashier turned his back completely.

The woman threw the hat down onto the counter, picked up her bag, and walked out of the store, grumbling.

Janna moved to the counter and reached for the hat. She looked at her money. Two weeks allowance plus feeding Mrs. Churchill's cats while she was in Iowa. An afternoon lost in a tale of adventure with a cup of hot chocolate, or a stranger's warm ears? She was eyeing the hat when it was taken from her hand.

"Popular item," the checkout man said, holding out his hand.

Janna paused a second, then handed him her money. He ripped the price tag in half and handed her back the hat. She checked to make sure that her mom was still occupied at the mitten and hat table and then ran out of the store. Janna blinked in the bright sun, trying to find the bag lady. For a woman with a cane, the bag lady certainly moved fast. When Janna caught sight of her, she was already more than a block away. Janna ran after her.

"Hey!"

The bag lady kept on walking. Janna ran faster.

"Hey, you!" she yelled. A number of people turned

around to look at Janna, but the bag lady wasn't one of them.

"Ma'am! Excuse me!" Janna called, but the woman just kept moving. Janna finally caught up with her and touched her arm.

The bag lady stopped and whirled toward Janna, her cane raised in the air.

"Leave me alone!" she yelled. Janna froze in shock. It was bad enough being yelled at in front of everyone on the street, but on top of that the bag lady was terrifying to look at. Her dark eyes were saddled by hairy caterpillar eyebrows, and the expression on her lined face made Janna think of gargoyles.

Janna held the hat out to her, breathless.

The bag lady just stared at it.

"Take it," Janna said. "It's for you."

The bag lady snatched it, a quick reptilian grab, a frog snagging a fly. The bag lady didn't look at the hat, didn't put it on, didn't say anything, just stared at Janna. Janna couldn't move. It was as if the woman's black eyes had anchored Janna to the pavement, and she knew without a doubt that this was a witch. A real witch who could cast a spell so that Janna would never be able to move again.

"Janna!"

She heard her mother from a long way away. The woman blinked and Janna felt the spell break.

"Janna?" Her mother's voice came again, closer this time.

Janna turned, nearly knocking down the pedestrian behind her, and walked quickly back to her mother.

"What are you doing out here?" her mother asked. "I'm done in there. Let's go to the bookstore."

"I don't have my money anymore. I lost it."

Janna felt her mother's eyes on her, but neither of them said anything further as they got back into Maybe.

As they drove away, Janna thought she saw a bobbing purple spot in the stream of people on the sidewalk, but she couldn't be sure.

Chapter 3

"I'm leaving now," Janna's mother called. "The school board meeting is in the gym. If you need me, I'll be there."

"Right," Janna said, looking out her bedroom window, through which she could see right into Elizabeth Newby's bedroom window.

Her mother walked down the hall to stand in Janna's doorway.

"Are you okay?" she asked. "You're awfully quiet."

"Just a little . . . tired," Janna said, still not looking at her mother.

Her mother was silent for a few seconds. "I know you didn't lose your money this morning."

"I know you know."

"Do you want to talk about it?"

"No."

"Right." Janna's mother still stood in the doorway. "It might be a long meeting, but I'll be home for dinner."

"Bye, Mom."

"Bye, sweetie."

After her mother left, Janna did her homework and chores. Then she took a cup of hot chocolate up to her room and sat on the bottom bunk of her bed. What she needed was a good book to sink into. Not just any book. She needed *The Secret Princess*. Sighing, Janna took the pink lottery ticket from beneath her pillow and tore it carefully into perfect fuzzy-edged squares. With each rip, she made a pronouncement.

"I will never buy another lottery ticket in my life."

Rip.

"I will be very, very rich when I grow up."

Rip.

"And then I will never buy used clothes again."

Rip.

"I will never, ever believe in good luck as long as I live."

Rip.

"That creepy old woman better appreciate her stupid purple hat," Janna said as she let the pink pieces flutter into her wastebasket.

"Oh, she does. I assure you, she does."

The voice came from above her. Janna looked up to see the bag lady sitting on the top bunk amid the stuffed toys. At least, it had to be the bag lady, for she was wearing the same purple coat and black galoshes, and if there had been any room for doubt, the unmistakable purple hat was perched atop her head.

Janna jumped up and backed away.

"What are you doing here? How did you get here?"

"I walked."

"No, how did you get *in* here? Into my room? Onto my bed?"

"I have my methods."

Janna stared at her. "How . . . did you find me? This is a long way from the thrift store."

"It wasn't easy. That's what took me so long, Janna. They're much more stringent about giving out information on minors now. And on a weekend, too!"

Janna narrowed her eyes. "How do you know my name?"

"It's what your mother called you, so I figured it was a safe guess."

"And who's *they*?"

The woman's eyes shifted, then she went on as if she hadn't heard Janna's question. "I came to thank you. You didn't give me a chance this morning."

"You frightened me!" Janna said.

"Well, you frightened me, too," the bag lady said, looking defensive.

"Me? How could I possibly frighten you?"

"Unexpected kindness is a very scary thing. I am accustomed to people who intend to make life difficult for me. That's why I yelled at you."

"Well, you're welcome for the hat." Janna paused. The bag lady hopped off the top bunk in a surprisingly fluid motion. She unbuckled her galoshes, which were oddly clean and dry given the weather, and with a couple of relieved grunts worked them off her feet. Then she went to Janna's closet door, opened it, and, shoving several pairs of Janna's shoes to one side, set her galoshes down beside them. Janna watched in stunned silence as the bag lady removed her hat and her coat, stuffed the hat tidily into one coat arm, and hung her coat up at the end of the closet rod. The bag lady closed the door, turned around, and smoothed out the front of her bulky gray sweater that fell over a shapeless emerald green dress. The bit of her legs that showed were clad in mismatched dancer's leg warmers, and below that Janna could see thick black socks. The black socks were worn through in several places, revealing another layer of socks, these bright red. The woman sighed in satisfaction and beamed at Janna expectantly.

"Well," she said.

Janna had no idea what that meant, but she knew things were getting a little strange.

"My mother isn't here, or I'm sure she would give you a ride back to . . . wherever. Would you like . . . a cup of hot chocolate before you go?"

"Oh, my, yes. That would be delightful, my dear. Nothing better to take the chill off old cold bones. But no rush. I'm very comfortable." With that, she hopped up onto the top bunk again, more easily than Janna was able to.

"I'll go make the cocoa now, so you can—" Janna hesitated. "Go home" seemed a little insensitive. "Get to where you need to be."

"Oh, I don't need to be any place other than where I am," the bag lady said brightly. "Not for a long time."

Janna stared at her. The bag lady stared back.

"And what do you mean by that?" Janna asked.

"What I mean, Janna," the bag lady said, "is that I'm not leaving."

Chapter 4

Janna stared at the woman, who leaned back on the bunk's pillow, crossed one leg over the other at the knee, and picked up a magazine.

"I . . . don't understand," was all Janna could manage.

"What part don't you understand?" The bag lady smiled, but her black bean eyes didn't. They glinted and burned deeply into Janna's own gray-blue ones. "To leave means to depart, which I am not going to do."

"I know you don't have a home, and when my mom comes back, she might be able to give you a ride, but . . . "

"I would love to meet your mother. Any chance she's near my size? And has some stylish clothes she might be tired of?"

"You can't stay here!"

The bag lady gestured. "There's plenty of room for two people in here. I've shared places this size with ten adults, and we didn't even have a bunk. You have no idea how little space I require. Why can't I stay here?"

"No way!"

"Surely you can share, just until spring."

Janna felt panic begin to make its trembling path through her body. "We don't have enough as it is."

"Oh, well, all the more reason for me to stay. I'll be a big help."

Janna backed herself toward the door. What she needed to do first was get out of the house, and then she had to call for help. But as Janna stared at the bag lady lying on her bed, she was suddenly gone, simply not there. Janna gasped, and then she bumped into something soft but solid behind her. She shrieked and whirled. There stood the bag lady, who reached out and grabbed Janna by the wrist.

"I'm sorry. I'm frightening you again. Please let me explain, and then, if you really want me to go, I will leave."

Janna forced herself to breathe slowly and speak calmly. "Please let go of me."

The bag lady instantly released Janna, and disappeared. Janna whirled to see the bag lady back on the top bunk.

"I will stay right here so as not to alarm you. I do not mean you any harm."

Janna stared. "How do you do that? Is it like some martial art or something?"

"Or something."

"Okay, you have five minutes to explain, and then you really are going to have to leave." Janna forced her words to be brave, but her voice wasn't.

The bag lady smiled, folded her hands primly, and leaned forward conspiratorially.

"I am a genie." She smiled wider, the lights in her black eyes shining brightly. Then she leaned back, arms folded, to watch the effect of her statement.

"A genie?" Janna repeated.

"You know, a *genie*." The bag lady looked a little irritated, as if she thought Janna was pretty dense.

She's nuts, Janna thought. *Completely berserk*.

"Can it be I have stumbled across the one American child over the age of two who is unaware of what a genie is? I am a jinn, a spirit capable of granting wishes!"

"You mean like Aladdin's genie?"

"Ah, I remember Al like it was yesterday." The bag lady smiled nostalgically.

"But why are you here, with me? I didn't find a lamp." *Gotcha*, Janna thought.

"Times have changed. We live where we choose." The bag lady patted her purple bag. "I contain myself in this charming and serviceable bag. Blends in with today's society a little better than a lamp, don't you think?"

Janna nodded. She knew better than to disagree with a crazy woman.

"Why me?"

"I belong to whomever displays an unselfish kindness to me." The bag lady harrumphed. "As you can imagine, I'm often a long time in between jobs."

"What about your last master?"

"Oh, he died," the bag lady said casually. "They often do."

"Died?" Janna's voice was a little shrill. "Why do they all die?"

"I didn't say they all die. I said they often die. But, actually, they do all die. Everybody dies, eventually, right?"

"What do they die of?"

"Excess, usually. Too much of too much isn't healthy, you know. I try to tell them that, but nobody ever listens."

"So, have you had a lot of masters?" Except for the bizarre topic, it almost sounded like a normal conversation to Janna's ears. Next they would be talking about the weather.

"Well, since someone must be kind to me to become my master, the pickings are a little slim, but how do you think Howard Hughes made his fortune? Or King Tut?"

"Bill Gates?"

"No. He was just the right person at the right time."

Janna was beginning to breathe a little more easily. Although wacko, the bag lady seemed harmless.

"So, do I get three wishes?"

"Oh, there's no limit on the number."

"My, you *are* generous." *Humor her, that's the right approach.*

"No, three has always been an artificial device to create tension in a story line. There never has been a limit. There are, however, some limitations."

"Provisos?" Janna grinned.

"Say what?"

"That's what Aladdin's genie calls them."

"The dude in the Disney film?" The bag lady sniffed. "Pure fabrication. Not reality-based at all. Anyway, as I was saying. One: I cannot create emotions. For example, I cannot directly make you happy, and I cannot directly make someone else miserable." She winked. "Of course, indirectly is an entirely different matter. Two: No blanket wishes, such as 'Make everybody nice to me.' Three: I cannot grant cash gifts in excess of twelve thousand dollars per year. That's straight from your American legal beagles—the tax hassles are unbelievable. In addition, I need you to sign this hold harmless agreement."

A piece of paper and a pen suddenly appeared in the bag lady's hand. She smiled apologetically as she held them out for Janna.

"Sorry, but the litigation potential is positively enormous." She cackled. "You know what they say—watch out, or you might get what you wish for!"

Janna reached for the paper. "This is gibberish."

The bag lady leaned over. "No, it's Farsi. Sorry."

The strange letters seemed to morph into English. Janna blinked.

"Whereas the party of the first part agrees to fulfill all explicitly expressed wishes, spoken or unspoken, to the extent of the party of the first part's abilities, subject to the limits of the clarity of the expression of said wishes, the party of the second part understands and agrees that such fulfillment of said wishes may have unintended consequences, not limited to death, destruction, and total chaos. . . ."

Blah, blah, blah.

Janna signed the paper.

"So, since you're so very poor, you'll be wanting some food, no doubt. Nothing worse than a belly hitting a backbone. So, food?"

"Um, okay."

"You have to *wish* for it, kid. Say, '*I wish for food.*'"

"Isn't that a little pedantic?"

"Rules is rules," the bag lady said.

"I wish for food," Janna repeated. Best to let this bizarre experience run its course.

The bag lady raised her chin and brought it down decisively. There was a slight *poof*, the sound of surrounding air being displaced, and a table laden with an impossible quantity of food appeared in front of Janna. She gasped and stepped back.

"How did you do that?"

"I'm not really sure. The physics of it escape me."

"You *are* a genie!"

The genie looked annoyed. "Shall we take it from the top?"

"No," Janna said. "I get it now."

"You're a little slower than my last master."

"Wow!" Janna moved around the table inspecting the large rounds of cheese, the meats, a whole pig with an apple in its mouth. She ran her hand over the exotic fruits, the gold-wrapped chocolates.

"Amazing! You're better than the lottery!"

"Gee, thanks." The genie seemed less than flattered.

"Take it away!" Janna said excitedly.

"Take it away?"

"I don't want any food. I want other stuff!"

"But . . . you said you wanted food."

"No, we have plenty to eat, but my mom buys only healthy stuff. Lots of fruits, veggies, whole grains. No soda or doughnuts or anything, unless it's for a special occasion."

The genie knit her brow. "So why do you call yourself poor?" She gestured around the room. "You have a nice place to live, warm clothes, food. Where's the poor part?"

"Well, I'd like to order out for pizza whenever I want to. Everybody else does. Do you know that I've never been to Disney World?" Janna continued, unaware of the odd look that crossed the genie's face. "I don't even have an iPod, *and* we don't get cable."

"How ever do you survive?" Janna thought she detected a note of sarcasm in the genie's voice.

They both fell silent, looking at each other. The genie sighed.

"So, poor little girl, what is your wish?"

"I want . . . No limit on the number of wishes now, right?"

The genie shook her head. "No, no limit."

"I want a wardrobe just like Elizabeth Newby's."

The bag lady stared at Janna. "How strange. Why in the world do you want that?"

"Because most of my clothes are secondhand, and I never get to go out and buy anything just because it's cool. It has to be practical, durable, appropriate, *and* not very expensive. Elizabeth Newby has the neatest clothes in the entire school, and I don't think she wears anything more than a couple times. Anything Elizabeth Newby wants, I want, so anything Elizabeth Newby has, give me."

"That's the very first thing on your list?"

"It's a start. Come on. I wish for you to take this all away, and I wish for Elizabeth Newby's clothes."

The genie shrugged. The table laden with food disappeared with another poofy displacement of air, except for a stray plate spinning on its edge.

"Sorry. I'm a little rusty, I guess."

Then the plate, with a slight squeak of surprise, was gone too, and Janna's room was instead filled with clothes.

Garments poured out of her closet. A jumble of jeans and shirts and sweaters were piled upon every surface; shoes covered her desk; socks and jackets and hats and jewelry were tangled together all over the floor. A pair of textured tights spun slowly from her bedroom ceiling fan. The genie struggled to sit up from under an enormous heap of strappy dresses, while swatting teenage lingerie from her face.

"Wow! I knew she was spoiled, but I had no idea . . . " Janna reached for the nearest sweater and held it up to herself in the mirror, then grabbed a hat and tried it on. "I look better in it than she does!

"Ooh! I've always loved this ring of hers." Janna slipped a chunky fake diamond onto her left ring finger.

Just then she heard Maybe in the driveway.

"Oh, no! My mother's home. Stay here. I'll be right back." After flinging the hat down, she ran out of her room and halfway down the hall before she remembered to come back and shut the door.

Chapter 5

Hi, Mom."

Janna's mother took off her coat and sagged down at the kitchen table, rubbing her forehead. She peered at Janna.

"You look a little . . . pink. And you're breathing funny. I hope you're not coming down with that bug that's going around."

"I'm fine," Janna said. Even if she had been inclined to, she wouldn't have known how to begin to tell her mother about the strange woman upstairs. Too late she remembered the ring and slid her right hand over her left. "How did the meeting go?"

"Not well at all. Berk Pizer got everyone worked up again about how high taxes are and how much money the school already gets. They're not going to pass the school budget this time either."

"But the classes are so overcrowded, and the building is falling apart," Janna said. "Not to mention that the teachers buy half the supplies themselves."

"I know, Janna, but too many people are worried about too little money, and Pizer plays on that fear so well." Carol shook her head. "I understand when people who are truly struggling are against an increase, but Berk Pizer is a very wealthy man. Why does he want to take away something as important as a good education from you kids? If everybody gave just a little more, it would make all the difference."

"Isn't he the head of the company you work at?"

"Yes." Janna's mother smiled slightly. "Fortunately, he doesn't have a clue that I work there. I don't think he likes the things I say very much."

A siren sounded outside, and they both jumped up as it turned down their street. A police car drove up to their house and came to a sudden stop, the siren squelching abruptly. Janna got a sick feeling (*how did they catch me so fast?*) as two uniformed men climbed out of the car. But instead of turning up the walk to Janna's house, they strode to the house across the street. She exhaled in relief.

"Oh, dear. Something has happened at the Newbys'. I should go over and see if I can help." Janna's mom grabbed her coat, and Janna reached for hers. Quickly they crossed the street and knocked on the door. Mr. Newby opened the door, looking rattled. They heard Mrs.

Newby shrieking from somewhere inside the house.

"We saw the police and wondered if you were okay. Can we help?"

Mr. Newby ran his hand through his hair and then beckoned them in.

"Elizabeth's run away!"

"Run away?"

"Strangest thing. Alice went upstairs to vacuum Elizabeth's room, and all her clothes were gone! Everything, not a sock in sight. She said she was going to the mall, but somehow she packed up everything and took it with her. Even her jewelry is missing!"

Feeling queasy, Janna stuffed her left hand into her coat pocket. She heard Mrs. Newby's shrill, frightened voice upstairs.

Janna's mother looked at her. "I think you should go home and I'd better stay with Alice. Will you be okay alone for a little bit?"

"Sure, I'll just go . . . um, finish up my homework."

Janna ran back to her house and up the stairs to her room. The genie sat serenely at Janna's desk, looking at a magazine, shaking her head in wonder or confusion, Janna wasn't sure which.

"You took Elizabeth's clothes!" Janna said.

"Of course I took her clothes. You told me to. She's a bit of a slob, don't you think?"

"Give them back!"

"You've changed your mind? Again? It usually takes a little longer for people to tire of their wishes. Although I admit that I was confused when after promising yourself you would never own used clothes again, that's the first thing you asked for."

"I can't have these clothes. They don't belong to me!"

"They do now."

"Give them back to her!"

"Everything?"

"*I wish for you to give all of Elizabeth Newby's stuff back to her.* Now!"

The room was immediately empty. Janna rubbed the spot on her finger where the beautiful ring had been yanked off.

"Why did you take them from her?"

"Where else would I get Elizabeth Newby's clothes?"

"Can't you just poof them?"

"Poof them?"

Janna stretched out her arms and made what she thought was a reasonable imitation of the noise that had accompanied the sudden arrival and departure of the food table in her room.

"I'm not getting your drift," the genie said. "Could you be a little more specific?"

"Just, you know, copy them and give them to me."

The genie scowled. "Copy them? Do I look like a Xerox machine? I can't do that. It defies the laws of nature."

"I'd say what you just did defies the laws of nature."

"Well, there are rules and then there are rules. Everything comes from someplace. There really is no free lunch. In order for me to give you something, I have to get it somewhere. Just as well you sent them back, though, because you're a bit porkier than Lizzie Newby."

"Sturdy. I'm sturdy," Janna replied, then looked at the genie in dismay as the implications set in. "Wait! How can I ever wish for anything if everything belongs to someone else?"

"I am neither a philosopher nor an ethicist, merely your humble servant." There was a glint in the genie's eye. "Anything else for today, dear? I'm a little weary after my first day back on the job."

"Yes, there is something else. I wish for an iPod loaded with the entire Beatles catalog. And a McDonald's fish sandwich and a large Coke."

"Do you want fries with that?"

"Sure."

The genie stared at Janna.

"I wish for fries with that."

"Poof?"

"Poof."

Instantly the items appeared on Janna's desk. Janna looked at the genie in annoyance. "Headphones, duh! I wish for a pair of headphones." At the genie's look, she added after a few seconds, "Please."

"The please is a nice touch, dear. Thank you."

A pair of headphones now rested neatly on the iPod.

"Where did these come from?"

"Do you really want to know?"

"No."

Janna opened the bag of food eagerly. The genie watched her for a moment.

"Do you have any idea how many people go to bed hungry each night?"

"No." Janna slurped her Coke.

"Don't talk with your mouth full," the genie snapped. "Do you know that the vast majority of the world will never, ever go to Disney World?"

"I don't care about the vast majority."

The genie paused. "No, I can see that you don't."

"What are you?" Janna asked. "Some kind of social reformer, like Jane Addams?" She had read about Jane Addams in school. "Or are you just trying to make me feel bad?"

The genie shook her head. "I've just been around a long time. Kind of changes your perspective on things."

"Good night," Janna said in dismissal.

The genie nodded. "Sleep tight."

With that the genie disappeared, but her plastic bag and cane remained. Janna tipped the bag carefully onto its side and slid both under her bed, out of sight. Janna ate her food quickly, and when she saw her mother come out of the Newbys,' she loudly sucked up the last of her soda and stuffed the garbage under her bed. Janna was carefully hiding the iPod in her nightstand when she heard her mother come into the house.

"Janna?"

"In here, Mom."

Carol walked into Janna's bedroom door, then stopped, sniffing.

"What?" Janna asked, a picture of innocence.

"Smells like grease."

Janna inhaled with exaggeration. "I don't smell anything."

Her mother shook her head as if to clear it.

"What's up across the street?" Janna asked, wondering how her wish and its reversal had been received at the Newbys', but not sure she really wanted to know.

"I went upstairs and found Alice in Elizabeth's room. It was the biggest mess I'd ever seen. Clothes everywhere! I can't imagine why they thought Elizabeth took anything at all. Alice was in the middle of it all, sobbing with her hands over her face. When she took her hands from her face and looked up, she started screaming. Then Elizabeth came home from the mall. I left Alice with Don and the cops, and I think she's still hysterical."

Indeed, if Janna listened carefully, she could hear little high-pitched sounds from across the street.

Her mother shook her head, looking dazed. "What a strange, strange night."

"Yeah," Janna agreed. *If you only knew*, she thought.

"It's late. I'll make us some dinner."

"I'm not really hungry."

"I want you to eat a little something anyway. I'll call you when it's ready." Carol sniffed the air again, and left with a puzzled look on her face.

Janna lay down on her bed, her mind whirling with the day's events. When her mother called her to eat, she pled an upset stomach. She really did feel a little woozy from all the excitement and confusion, not to mention how quickly she had gobbled her fish sandwich and fries. After her mother said good night and went to her own room, Janna put the headphones on, curled up with her new music, and covered up with her quilt. Through her window she watched Elizabeth and her mother hanging up dresses and folding sweaters. Janna held the iPod in her hand. Turning it over, she saw the initials R.E.J. etched in the hard plastic. What was R.E.J. doing tonight without his/her music?

"Hey, genie," she whispered, but no one replied.

Janna sighed, took off the headphones, and hid everything in her night table. She pulled the genie's purple bag out from under the bed and dumped the contents onto the floor. There was a clear zippered bag, and inside it was a comb, a toothbrush, and a small tube of toothpaste like you get at the dentist's. There were three pairs of socks, two pairs of old lady underpants so gray that Janna held them between finger pincers, a plastic poncho, a small child's blanket, a pocketknife, an empty water bottle, and a small carved wooden box that wouldn't open no matter how hard she tried to pry up the lid. That was all. Janna packed everything back into the bag and crawled back into bed. She lay awake a long time before going to sleep.

Chapter 6

When Janna awoke, the genie was sitting at her desk reading the latest pop culture magazine.

"Give it back," Janna said.

"Give what back?" The genie sounded as innocent and sweet as a benevolent aunt, albeit a pretty ratty-tatty one.

"The iPod. To R.E.J., whoever that is. I wish you to return it."

The genie raised her eyebrows. "Done."

Janna resisted the urge to whip open the drawer of her nightstand to check.

"And the McDonald's, shall I give that back too? Although that presents a slightly trickier problem."

"No, I'll keep that, thank you."

"Next time, don't stuff your food garbage under the bed. The smell drove me crazy all night."

"You were under my bed? All night? Isn't that . . . illegal or something?"

"No, but littering is."

"It's *my* room, so it's not littering."

"It's still very piggy. What would your mother say?"

The genie had a point. Janna's mom would ask some difficult questions if she found the remnants of Janna's dinner, since there wasn't a McDonald's within walking distance.

"You're right. Could you get rid of the McDonald's garbage for me?"

"Get rid it? And just where shall I put it?"

"I don't care—away!"

"Are you aware of the tremendous landfill problem in this country? There is no 'away.'"

"Just get rid of it!"

"Do the poof thing?"

"Yes, poof!"

Nothing happened. Janna looked at the genie. The genie looked back.

"I *wish* for you to get that bag of trash out of my house. *Jeesh.* Picky, picky, picky."

Janna was staring out the window when the bag appeared on Maybe's hood.

"Hey! I said get rid of it."

"*Jeesh.* Picky, picky, picky." The bag lady frowned, but the bag disappeared.

Janna turned to face her. "Okay, I've been thinking about this. When I ask for something, don't get it from anyone I know. And there can't be any names on the stuff. It needs to be brand-new."

"Where am I supposed to steal new stuff?"

"Steal? You're granting my wish; you're not stealing."

"You're right. I'm granting the wish: You're the one stealing."

"I am not. Why all this guilt-tripping? Nobody ever guilt-tripped Aladdin."

"Aladdin was a story. This is real."

Janna frowned. "I thought you said you remembered Aladdin."

"Everybody remembers Aladdin. I first heard the story on my own mother's knee. It's sort of like 'The Three Little Pigs' for baby genies."

"Speaking of baby genies, what's your real name?" Janna asked.

"Name?"

"Like, what should I call you? It's a little awkward to holler *'You! Bag lady!'*"

"Hmm. That's a problem."

"A problem? How can asking your name present any kind of a problem?"

"Well, it's the use it or lose it concept, I'm afraid, dear, and I just haven't been using my name much lately."

"Use it or lose it? You mean, you lost your name?"

"Well, forgot it, anyway."

"You forgot your own name?"

"Hey, talk to me when you're my age and we'll see how much you remember. If it makes you feel any better, you can call me whatever you like. Within reason."

Janna thought for a moment. "Your new name is Eugenie."

"Isn't that the same as '*You! Bag lady!*'?"

"It's different. Trust me."

The genie rolled her eyes. "Why not one of those popular new names? Brittany? Tiffany?"

"Believe me, you don't look like either a Brittany or a Tiffany. Or even an Ashley."

Eugenie brandished the magazine she had been reading. "Maybe Paris?"

Janna ignored her and pressed some booklets toward her.

"Okay, Eugenie, here's a few catalogs. These companies have warehouses, right? I'm not taking anything from any little kid. I'm not taking anything from someone who will miss it. I'm taking from wealthy business people. Just get me everything that I've marked with a check in these catalogs, colors and sizes as indicated."

"How do you know they're wealthy?" the bag lady asked.

"They have this stuff and I don't. That is my definition of wealthy," Janna said.

Eugenie flipped through the catalogs. "And you . . . happened to have these all ready, just in case?"

"Well, actually, yes."

Eugenie held up a page and pointed. "Do you *really* need one of these sweaters in every color?"

Janna set her chin. "Eugenie, I wish for you to bring to me one of everything I've indicated in these catalogs, of appropriate size and color. Will that do?"

"Fine. You asked for it," Eugenie said.

"Couldn't you at least say something a little more genie-like?"

Eugenie sighed. "Your wish is my command."

The room instantly became full of boxes, so many that Janna didn't even have room to blink. There were boxes on her feet, boxes smashed up against her back, boxes jammed to the ceiling, boxes all around her, boxes on top of her, crushing her.

"I can't breathe, Eugenie! Get rid of the boxes! Unpoof! Quick! Quick!" Janna took a breath. "I wish for you to get rid of all this stuff!"

Immediately, her room was clear.

"No!" Janna shrieked.

Eugenie looked at her in exasperation. "Do you want these things or not? It's a *little* difficult for me to tell."

"Bring the stuff back, this time without the boxes."

"Everything in the warehouse was in boxes. I wanted

you to be aware it was all brand-new." Eugenie spoke a little stiffly.

"Then take everything out of its box before you bring it here."

Eugenie glared at Janna. "I'm getting a little tired of being a returns clerk. Are you quite sure this time?"

"Yes! I wish for everything back, but without the boxes."

Janna's room filled once more, but at least this time there was breathing room.

"Wow!" Finally she had gotten it right. Janna whooped when she saw the endless jumble of things. She picked up a pair of inline skates, then dropped them to squeeze a large teddy bear. Quickly, breathlessly, Janna ran her hand over the latest in downhill skis, a chemistry set, a lava lamp, sports clothes. And there was the entire Medieval Maid series! Every game she knew about, and a few she didn't, was stacked atop her desk. Neat knickknacks, cool baubles, and assorted garments covered every square inch of her room.

"Excuse me for asking," Eugenie said, holding up one of the catalogs Janna had given her to order from, "but did you really have every single item in this one checked?"

Janna ignored her. Eugenie picked up a red tricycle. "And just what, may I ask, are you going to do with this?"

Janna grabbed a new backpack, but at a sudden thought, her face fell.

"How am I going to explain to my mom where I got all this stuff?"

"N-M-P," Eugenie said, then turned to stare out the window in supreme disinterest.

"Excuse me?"

"Not. My. Problem."

"How did your other masters work it out?"

"I don't recall King Tut worrying about what his mommy thought."

Janna sighed and surveyed her riches. "What good is all of this if I have to hide it?"

Eugenie looked at her. "Why do you have to hide it?"

"My mom would make me give it back."

"Why?" Eugenie tilted her head and looked at Janna intently.

"She thinks you should earn the things you have, because if you don't, then you don't value them."

"Call me curious, but if your mother could have anything she wanted, what would your mother ask for?"

"World peace or something stupid like that."

"Yeah, pretty lame." Janna could not miss the sarcasm in Eugenie's voice this time.

"How about a new car for my mom?"

"How are you going to explain that to her?"

"I could say I won it. No, wait! I've got a great idea! How about if I just win the lottery?"

"Oh, you already have."

"Already? Poof, huh?" Janna laughed and, in spite of herself, hugged Eugenie. "You are amazing! What do I do now? Don't I need the winning ticket to collect my money? How much did I win?"

"Not that lottery. Remember last winter when you and your mom were driving down the interstate in that whiteout?"

"Yeah, we hit ice and Maybe spun out of control into a ditch. There was a semi coming and it missed us by about a centimeter! I thought we were going to get creamed."

"Life is a series of lotteries, Janna. You've won a lot of them."

"You mean . . . I haven't won the Mega Multimillion Dollar Lotto Lottery?"

"You don't want to. Do you know what happens when people win the lottery?"

"They live happily ever after."

"Actually, they often don't. Many end up worse off, because they thought all that was wrong with them was that they didn't have enough money. Maybe there was nothing wrong with them at all, but they thought there was."

"Well, there's nothing wrong with me that being filthy rich won't take care of, okay?"

"That's what they all say."

"I'll be different."

"I've heard that one before too. It's easy to pretend that the reason you're grumpy, the reason you're overweight, all comes back to too little money. Maybe it comes back to too little, but not too little money."

"I don't think you're in the proper spirit here," Janna said.

"Likewise."

They sat in an unfriendly silence for a moment, until Janna turned to Eugenie with a suspicious look on her face.

"If you can make all this stuff appear in my room, why do you wear those ratty clothes and sleep in the streets?"

"Simple. I'm not my own master. Genies like me must survive on the milk of human kindness. As you can see, the milk is down to a few dribbles at this point in civilization."

"But I can make wishes for you, can't I?"

Eugenie shrugged. "Sure."

"I wish you to wish for whatever you want. Go ahead. Poof!"

Eugenie looked at Janna. "Thank you. That's the second kindness you've shown me."

Janna waited expectantly. "Well?"

"Okay, poof."

Janna looked at Eugenie and around her room. Seeing nothing different, she took Eugenie's plastic bag and dumped it upside down onto her bed.

"It's the same pathetic stuff!" Janna cried. "Where are the nice clothes? The money? The goodies?"

"I didn't wish for clothes or money. Or, as you say, *goodies.*"

"Why not? What is it that you want more?"

"It's not what I want; it's what I need. Want is a passing pang. Need is a big deep hole that you can't get around or through until it is filled up."

"All right, all right. What do you need?"

"I need a warm, safe place to live for the rest of the winter."

"I told you, you can't stay here."

"But you said I could do the poof thing, so now I can."

Janna closed her eyes. "My mother will kill me."

"I doubt it. Mothers don't kill their children nearly as often as they should."

"Humpf," Janna said. Then she saw the time. She stood quickly. "Can you, like, make all these things invisible, or something?"

"What's the point of invisible possessions?"

"I need to leave in a few minutes and I can't chance my mom seeing this stuff. In fact, whenever my mom is home, I wish for it all to be invisible." There was no poof, but everything she had wished for disappeared. Janna was pleased with her solution.

She headed for the door, but stumbled over something

she couldn't see that had hard pointy edges. Stopping, she rubbed her elbow and turned to eye the genie, who was following her.

"Do you . . . have to go wherever I go?"

"No, but I do love to get out and about. What if you have an emergency whim or a crisis of consumption that just can't wait? Especially if you're going to the mall, you could just do the princess point-and-poof act."

"I'm not going to the mall. I'm going to a friend's house. Just stay here and keep quiet, okay?"

"What's the matter? Are you ashamed of me?"

"I'm just not sure how to explain you."

"You could introduce me as your great-aunt or some such."

"I've known Albert since before dirt. He's met all my relatives by now."

"Introduce me as your genie, then."

"Just stay here, okay?"

"I don't have to. You're not the boss of me."

Janna shouldered her backpack and navigated carefully to her bedroom door.

"Actually, I think I am," she said firmly, sounding to her own ears a little like her mother.

*

Janna walked the three blocks to Albert DellaRosa's house. She had walked the three blocks to Albert's house more days in her life than she hadn't. They never called each other, just wandered in and out of each other's homes like house pets. Albert walked to her house some days too, but Albert, who was legally Albert III, and his father, Albert II, known as Albertoo, had always had better entertainment options than Janna and her mother, so generally Janna ended up at the DellaRosas'. Besides better entertainment options, Albert possessed something else Janna lacked—a strong aptitude for math. Janna's geometry test was tomorrow, and only Albert could crack through Janna's stubborn insistence that (a) math was a waste of time and (b) she could not learn math.

Albertoo was an accountant, and Janna assumed that Albert had received his disproportionate amount of math smarts from his father. What she couldn't figure out was why somebody so good at crunching numbers wasn't rich. Janna had once asked her mother about it.

"What makes you think they're not rich?" Janna's mother had said, not even looking up from what she was doing.

"Mom! They drive a car not much newer than Maybe. And I know Albert wanted to go to nerd camp last year and his dad couldn't afford it. You *know* Albertoo would send Albert to a place like that if at all possible. Heck, Albertoo would probably go with him!"

"Nerd camp? Please tell me there really isn't such a thing."

"There is! Albert showed me the brochure. The camp T-shirts have pockets, so of course they get pocket protectors with the camp logo on them."

"Of *course*. But what do you do at nerd camp? I take it you don't scratch bug bites and braid lanyards?"

"Mom! You live in dorms and take college classes with a bunch of other really bright kids."

"A bunch of other really bright *affluent* kids, it sounds like."

"Well, yeah."

"Sounds a little, um, un-summerlike."

"Well, they do have some forced social activities, you know, so you have to interact with other nerds."

"Forced social activities, like . . . ?"

"I don't know, mandatory fun stuff. You can't not have fun. Ask an affluent nerd. Anyway, why doesn't Albertoo have more money? Tiffany Cram's mom is an accountant too, and she drives a Volvo. A new one. With heated seats."

"Well, for one thing, Albertoo is a very honest man." Janna had thought perhaps Mrs. Cram had been insulted, but she hadn't been sure. "And for another, he only handles nonprofit organizations."

"So he could be rich and he's not? That sounds a little less than bright."

"Maybe he *feels* rich," Carol had said, and Janna had felt a small beam of disapproval emanating from the mothership.

"Humpf," Janna had replied in her defense, but she had dropped the subject.

Chapter 7

Janna arrived at the DellaRosas' smallish cedar shake house, knocked her special knock—tap tap tap *thud*—and, without waiting for a response, walked in.

"Hi, Albertoo," she said to the pale dark-haired man sitting at a computer in a corner of the living room. His legs were crossed at the knees, his khaki pants belted up somewhere around his armpits over a white shirt. His sharp face peered closely at the computer screen as if it contained all the secrets ever whispered and he were a little hard of hearing. His hair was thinning and slicked back, his glasses dark-rimmed and a little on the thickish side. They were actually quite trendy, but Janna knew that this was only because the retro look was back in style, as the glasses frames were the same ones in the picture on the buffet of Mr. and Mrs. Albertoo's wedding. Albert's mother wore similar glasses in the picture, but Janna didn't know if Mrs. Albertoo would have updated her eyewear over the years or not. Mrs. Albertoo had passed away years ago, and Janna could barely remember her.

"Hello," Albertoo said, not bothering to look at her. He wasn't being rude—Janna was convinced that Albertoo was incapable of even thinking something rude. He was the kind of man whose strongest curse was "Sugar!" and if you said the word "ass" in front of him, he would look at you and say "Language!" in a mildly shocked voice. If he had been asked under oath if Janna was present in the house, he would no doubt have denied it and passed any lie detector test, simply because he was on auto-Albertoo. Albertoo just got occupied and disappeared from the normal mortal space-time continuum. It was a wonder he hadn't lost Albert when he was little, Janna's mother had said more than once, "lost" meaning: leave Albert at the day care, the grocery, the pediatrician's. Survival of the fittest, she had said, presumably meaning Albert, not Albertoo.

Janna walked up the stairs to the study, where she knew she would find Albert in front of a computer screen teeming with odd animated creatures doing odd animated-creature things. She supposed Albert would grow up to look like his father, but for now his dark hair was wildish and long, and if it had a tendency to look as if he hadn't brushed it, it was because he hadn't. His glasses were identical to his father's, and outside of Albertoo only Janna knew that Albert's vision was fine. He just liked the way the glasses looked—this was the only indication Janna had ever seen that Albert even knew what he looked like. If his ripped jeans were already belted up around his armpits, that fact was undetectable beneath a worn and baggy T-shirt. The rips in his jeans were not a fashion statement, fashion being something outside both of the DellaRosa gentlemen's sphere of understanding. There was simply no one around to notice the rips, or care. Janna sat down on the futon behind Albert without saying anything and pulled out her math book.

"Define pi," he said.

"Umm, three something."

Albert turned around and faced her. "Three point one four, for general purposes. You can take it out forever, and it will never repeat. Isn't that cool?"

Janna squinted at him.

"Now, what is pi?" Albert asked.

"Pi is a stupid number."

Albert looked personally offended. "Don't say such a thing. Pi is a very important concept! Where would the world be without an understanding of pi?"

"About where it is right now, I imagine."

"Somebody's grumped. Let's start over: I asked you to define pi and you told me its value. But what does pi *represent*?"

"You mean what is the essence of pi?"

"Janna, I *do* have other things to do, even if you don't."

"Like take pi out to a bazillion places?"

Albert stared down his nose at her and turned back to his computer.

"Okay, okay, let me think. . . . It has something to do with the radius of a circle."

"Circumference, not radius. It's the ratio of the circle's circumference to its diameter."

"I hate this! I memorized that last week, and now it's like I've never heard it!"

"Don't memorize—*understand*! Understanding is more efficient and actually easier than memorizing."

"How can anybody understand something like pi?"

"Think of it this way." Albert took a strip of paper and taped the ends together to make a circle. He took another piece of paper and trimmed it to fit the diameter of the circle, then untaped the circle and held the two pieces of paper up side by side. "See? It takes about three of the diameter to make the circumference."

He held the two strips out to her.

Janna sighed and looked away.

"If you flunk this test, you might have to repeat the class." Albert looked stern, at least for Albert. He took the longest piece of paper and twisted it, then taped it into a Möbius strip. Janna had been fascinated the first time she had seen him do this, and it still entranced her to watch Albert trace his finger around the magic loop. In spite of herself, she reached her finger up to follow the tail-eating paper path too.

"It's no use. I can't concentrate today. I don't know what's wrong with me." Well, she did, but . . . "Why don't you just give me your old test from when you took the class? You know Mr. Callahan never changes them much."

"That would be—," Albert started.

"Dishonest," they both finished.

"I wish your scruples were more relaxed," Janna said.

"And I wish your laziness was less legion." Trust Albert to make her run to the dictionary to decipher an insult. "You'll do fine. I don't know why you don't think you can do it. You're smart enough, you're just lazy. Some things in life you do have to try at, Janna."

"You sound like my mom."

"Maybe you should listen to her."

"You're in my age cohort, you're not supposed to say things like that. Besides, you've known me since before I had teeth—have I ever listened to her?"

"Nope." Albert sighed. "You know, my mom and dad knew each other since they were babies too. They were born on the same day in the same year and their moms shared a hospital room. Isn't that weird?"

"Yes, Albert. We've agreed a gabillion times before that it is weird." Next he would say that Albertoo always knew he would marry Albert's mom.

"My dad says he always knew he would marry my mom. He thinks the best long-term relationships start early."

They sat in silence a moment.

"Albert, if you could have anything in the world, what would it be?"

He considered. When Albert considered, his eyes got a little unfocused. (When he considered really hard, he closed them.) After a moment he nodded.

"A new computer."

"No! I mean if you had absolutely no limits on what you could have. Think big, really big, Albert."

"Okay. How about a really big new computer. Gigs and googols of ram and disk. And . . . a huge high-quality graphics screen!" He looked at Janna sideways, eyes a little wide, to see if he had gone too far.

"You're not trying."

"I'm not?"

"How about . . . two computers?"

"What would I do with two computers? Wait . . . Can I give one to my dad?"

"You are truly clueless." Janna tried another tack. "What would you do if you had a lot of money? I mean scads and scads of money."

"Stock mutual funds, about seventy percent. Even though they're a little volatile, over the long haul they outperform any other investment vehicle."

"If you had scads and scads of money, you'd invest it?" She had known Albert all her life, but he never failed to amaze her several times a week.

"Of course. You're never too young to plan for retirement, Janna."

"What if you had sooooo much money you could buy all the stocks you could ever dream of and still have money left over?"

"Oh!" He looked relieved, and a gleam entered his eye. "That's different, way different."

Janna looked up; Albert might still come through.

"I'd prefund my college account. Possibly set up a revocable trust. Maybe pick up a few pet stocks, just for grins."

"Albert, you are hopeless. What would your *dad* do with that much money?"

"Well, he's a lot older, so I expect he'd cut the stocks back to around fifty percent and increase the bonds and maybe add some T-bills. That's after he totally funded both our IRAs and paid off the mortgage. That's *probably* what he would do, but we could ask him if you want to be sure." Albert gestured toward the door.

Janna looked at him. Albert looked back. Janna looked at him until he looked over his shoulder as if there might be someone else behind him she was fixing with that strange stare. When he saw there wasn't, Albert raised his hands in a *What?* gesture.

Janna sighed. Why did she like Albert? Albert was . . . just Albert. They'd been buds since before they had started laying down permanent memories, temperaments set in stone even then: Albert quiet, methodical, placid; Janna a little intense and prone to fits of pique, always concerned she was missing out on something somewhere. *Remember when your diaper exploded in the wading pool at preschool, Albert? Yeah, and remember when you had that hissy fit in kindergarten because you couldn't have the yellow place mat at snack time and you hauled off and hit Gail Goldstein and got sent home? Well, at least I didn't have to get carted to the emergency room the way you did because you believed Gretchen Hudson when she told you it was good luck to stick jelly beans up your nose.* There was never a time before Albert. So it really didn't matter that he was exasperating and annoying and nerdy and odd. He was just Albert. Someday he would look just like his dad and probably have a son just like himself. Janna shuddered. She hoped it would be a son; a female version of Albert would be . . . unthinkable.

Chapter 8

Math was the last period of the day, so Janna had plenty of time to contemplate her impending spectacular failure. She had given up on Albert the day before (or rather, he had given up on her) and had returned home to discover that Eugenie was nowhere to be found. She had tried wishing out loud, but nothing had happened, and the genie didn't show up Monday morning either.

By the time two thirty rolled around, Janna had worked herself into a fair tizzy about her math exam, bouncing between being fairly certain she could pull it off if she just tried hard enough to being quite certain that she should just call her entire mathematics career off at the end of eighth grade. The truth was, both Albert and her mother were right: She was plain lazy. Math was the only subject that didn't come easily to her, and for that reason alone she resented it. Why was it her fault? Maybe it was the book's fault—or Mr. Callahan's? Why should *she* have to work at *it*? Why couldn't math just—behave? Where most people might develop some discipline, Janna developed an attitude. By the time she was sitting in Mr. Callahan's geometry class with a two-page test, her attitude was the most functioning part of her.

I can't do this, she said to herself when she saw the first problem. *No problem. I'll just come back to it.* She looked at the next problem. *I can't do this one either.* She closed her eyes and tried to recall the explanations Albert had stepped through again and again. She knew diameter and radius were related somehow—how did that go? After a few minutes she was convinced that she recognized most of the words, but the concepts flitted off, laughing at her. After at least several minutes she gave up any delusions that she could ace the test; she now thought only of avoiding failing it. Just 60 percent would do it. She skimmed over the test and realized 60 percent was beyond the realm of possibility. She not only couldn't remember any geometry but seemed to have forgotten basic arithmetic as well. She sat blankly as the rest of the students scribbled, scratched their heads, stared at the ceiling for inspiration, scribbled some more. She was in the midst of a fine and comprehensive brain freeze the likes of which she had never experienced before. Her mind stepped outside of her body; she could hear every move of the second hand on the silent wall clock. Time assumed a strange proportion as she reviewed the problems one by one and ascertained without a doubt that none caused even a flicker in the maze of her math mind. She knew she should be able to do at least three quarters of them respectably, knew she had solved similar ones for homework and had made a decent, if less than stellar, showing on them. But not today. Her thoughts wandered to a nice time she and her mother had had at the beach last year. Her mind needed to grasp something and she was relieved to find this rather pleasant memory still in there. Too bad it was quite unrelated to the shapes and truly irritating equations on the pages before her.

Mr. Callahan looked up occasionally, and she gave a credible imitation of the thinking-writing-thinking process. Oh, poop, the fifty-minute class was almost done. People were checking their work, or sitting quietly, pencils down, their countenances clear and untroubled. She hated each and every one of them. Janna could hear both Albert's words and her mother's when they saw the large and perfect zero on this test. Well, maybe not a zero, since most teachers gave a point or two for putting your name on the paper. Janna went back and carefully added her middle initial to her name on the first page, just in case it was worth an extra half point.

At least she wouldn't have to deal with the fall-out today—they handed the tests in facedown, and her incompetence would be hidden for a while. She wished the answers would just appear on her exam. She wished—oh, double poop—*the answers had just appeared on her exam*! She gasped, and several people, including Mr. Callahan, looked at her. She bent her head over the exam and began to erase the numbers that were, eerily, in her very own handwriting. Then she stopped. Why? She hadn't deliberately wished for the answers, but now that it had happened . . . In fact, this opened up a whole new perspective on school for Janna. The bell rang. Janna gave Mr. Callahan a sweet smile as she turned her test in. Then she went home.

She was setting the table for dinner when Albert walked into the house. He had a special knock too—*thud* tap tap tap—but he didn't use it this time. In fact, he didn't knock at all. Had Janna's mom been home, he might have knocked, but from the look on his face, maybe not.

"*What did you think you were doing?*"

Janna hadn't seen Albert quite this way before, but she guessed it was called adolescent-boy-angry.

"What do you mean?" She asked, though she suddenly knew precisely what he meant. She had forgotten that Albert was making money this year correcting papers for Mr. Callahan.

"What did you hope to gain by cheating?"

"What makes you think I cheated?" It sounded

unconvincing even to her ears, and Albert knew her better than she knew herself.

"Because you got a perfect score on it. You didn't know it last night, so you sure didn't know it this afternoon. *Ergo*, you cheated."

"There are other explanations."

"Like?"

Janna looked at him. He was as angry as he had been when he had seen Mrs. Hester across the street hit her dog with a broom. Mrs. Hester was a little afraid of Albert now, and so was Janna.

"Like . . . you're a good teacher?" But she winced as she said it. It was really low to manipulate your friends. "Or . . . I really *am* smart." Was manipulating better or worse than lying? She wasn't sure.

"I *am* a good teacher, and you are smart, but I'm not that good, and you're lazy. In fact, you were too lazy to even cheat right!"

"There's a right way to cheat?" How could there be a right way to do the wrong thing?

"The best cheaters know enough to not get a perfect score! They mess up on at least one of the hardest problems."

Janna realized she didn't know enough to even recognize the hardest problems. They were *all* impossible. But this probably wasn't the time to bring that up.

"I. Didn't. Cheat. I promise."

"I. Don't. Believe. You. I promise."

They glared at each other.

"Janna, not understanding something is acceptable. Not studying enough is less acceptable, but you only hurt yourself. Cheating isn't acceptable *at all*. You didn't gain anything by acing that test. In fact, you *lost* something. You're a better person than that. I don't know what you were thinking."

Janna looked at him. She had cheated. She had known it was cheating all along. But she didn't know how to begin with Albert. It turned out she didn't have to.

"You're going to tell Mr. Callahan tomorrow. Or I will." Albert turned around and walked out the door, slamming it. Albert slamming a door. Now, that was a first.

Janna stared at the back of the door for a moment, then walked up to her bedroom, which was again cluttered with her wish booty. Eugenie was reading *The Secret Princess* on the top bunk.

"Where have you been?" Janna asked.

"I have Sundays off. I'm not your slave, you know."

"But you are!"

"Not since we unionized in the 1900s."

"Well, where were you this morning?"

Eugenie's eyes slid away from Janna's. "I was under the bed. I'm . . . not really a morning person."

"You were slacking," Janna said. "Besides, it's creepy that you sleep under my bed."

Eugenie shrugged. "I'm afraid of falling off the top bunk."

"You never told me I could wish for things without you being present."

Eugenie shrugged. "You didn't ask."

"That's lame, and you know it."

"You could have unwished it. Or erased the answers, or modified them, or—"

"You should have warned me."

Eugenie just looked at her.

"Albert is furious with me."

"Of course he is. You know how he is about cheating."

"Yeah, I do. But . . . how do you know?"

Eugenie stuck out her tongue. "Magic. Nyah-nyah."

"But I didn't mean to cheat!"

"You could have unwished the answers, but you didn't, so there was intent. And it's not the method that determines a crime, it's the intent."

"So what am I supposed to do now?"

"How about tell him the truth?"

"The truth? Gee, Albert, I have a genie living under my bed and I didn't know wishes worked remotely, and I panicked on the test and wished I had the answers. And all of a sudden, I did."

"There. Was that so hard?"

"Why do I have to explain anything to him? He's just Albert. Why do I care what he thinks?" A thought occurred to her. "Is there anything else you haven't warned me about? Maybe I should look again at that paper I signed. I didn't read the fine print."

Eugenie looked at her. "Wishes is wishes. If it comes out of your mouth or into your mind in the form of a wish, it counts. Except on my day off."

"Meaning?"

"Meaning, I wouldn't be singing songs about being an Oscar Mayer wiener."

"You really enjoy twisting me up in knots, don't you?"

Eugenie didn't respond, but there was a small smile on her face when she turned back to the book.

They heard the door open downstairs.

"My mom's home!"

"Janna?" Her mother called.

"Coming, Mom."

"Quiet!" Janna hissed to Eugenie. "And make all this stuff invisible! How many times do I have to tell you?" She walked out to greet her mom.

"Everything okay?" Carol Danner asked.

"Sure. I mean, why wouldn't it be?"

"Albertoo called me just as I was leaving work. He said Albert was slamming doors and he had the distinct idea it had something to do with you."

"Albert slamming doors? That—um—boggles the mind."

"Precisely. He said Albert even refused to play Risk with him, he was so upset."

"That's pretty—critical."

Carol looked at Janna and nodded. She took a step away toward the stairs, and then turned back.

"I know that Albert and Albertoo seem like they're tuned in to a different frequency sometimes, but they are both thoroughly decent people—so decent that they just rise above the mess of it all. That's very rare."

"I'm not sure what you're saying, Mom."

"I'm saying that I hope you haven't been . . . mean to Albert."

"It's just Albert. He's such a . . . *nerd*."

"You say that like it's a bad thing." Her mother crossed her arms and looked at Janna. "Albert's the sweetest person on earth, and you know it. If you have done something to upset him, both you and I know what you're going to have to do next."

Chapter 9

After dinner Janna sighed and looked at herself in the mirror. *Liar. Cheat.* She sighed again and walked the three blocks to Albert's house. Tap tap tap *thud*, and she walked in. Albertoo wasn't in his regular position at the computer. She walked upstairs to the study and found Albert facing his computer and Albertoo sitting on the futon staring forlornly at the neatly arranged Risk game board on the table in front of him, his hands folded in his lap. He brightened as Janna walked into the room, the glum look on his face fading somewhat.

"Albert! Look who's here!" he said, voice too loud, too hearty. Albert grunted.

"Hey, Janna!" Albertoo said.

Janna jumped.

Albertoo grinned, way too wide. "How do you drive an accountant bonkers?"

Janna shook her head.

"Tie his hands together, and then fold up a road map the wrong way in front of him!" Albertoo guffawed and slapped his knee.

Janna raised her eyebrows.

"Why did the accountant stare at his glass of orange juice for three hours?"

Janna said nothing.

"Because the label said *concentrate.* Ha! Ha, ha, ha!"

Janna stared at him and managed a pathetic smile. Albert stayed facing the computer, silent.

Albertoo tried again. "How about if we have a geometry party like we used to when you guys were in the single digits? You know, square crackers, triangular-shaped cheese, and circular pepperoni?"

The following silence was loud and painful.

"Want to go for a walk, Albert?" Janna said.

"It's dark and getting colder. Why don't you stay in?" Albertoo fussed. "I'll make us hot chocolate with marshmallows! Remember, you guys get your age in marshmallows! That's a *lot* of marshmallows!"

Albert and Janna both looked at him.

"Fine. Go for a walk," Albertoo said. "I'll just go . . . run a few numbers."

Albert didn't look at her as he put on his coat, opened the door, and walked out. They didn't look at each other as they walked down the sidewalk, Albert presumably because he was angry and Janna because she thought it would be easier to talk to him if she didn't look at him. It wasn't.

"I didn't cheat, Albert."

"So how do you explain one hundred percent on a test that if I gave it to you right now you would not be able to manage ten percent?" Albert finally turned and fixed her with a hard look, a look she had never been on the receiving end of, a look heretofore reserved for dog broomers. She didn't like it. He somehow wasn't just Albert anymore. There was a glimpse of someone else there, a less kind and gentle Albert, a darker Albert. Albert Vader.

"Well, I cheated, but I didn't mean to cheat."

He didn't respond. He was not going to make this easy for her.

"It all started on Saturday when I went to the thrift store with my mom." Albert knew she wore secondhand clothes—he was the only one that she didn't mind knowing. "There was this lady, and she really, really needed this hat but didn't have enough money. She was saying that her ears were freezing off, and you know how much I hate being cold. Nobody ought to have to be cold, so I bought the hat for her.

"Anyway, it turns out she wasn't just any old lady, but a genie—like, a real genie, you know—lamps and stuff but she uses this tacky plastic shopping bag, and because I gave her the hat, now she's *my* genie—like, she grants my wishes, and when I was sitting at that test and didn't know anything, I wished the answers would appear, and they did, but it wasn't a real wish—it was an accidental wish, but why change it? You know?"

Janna took a breath, deeply, and in a strange moment of clarity realized exactly what Ms. MacKenzie, her English teacher, meant by a run-on sentence. She looked at Albert hopefully, but his forehead had gotten a little wrinkled and he was looking at her strangely.

"You don't believe me, do you?" And she suddenly knew how hard life was going to be if Albert didn't believe her. If Albert stopped being her friend, the world was going to be a very lonely place. In spite of their very different personalities, through all her temper fits and their petty disagreements over the years, Albert had never once taken back his friendship, because that's what real friendship is. But Janna understood somehow that even the best and oldest and most tolerant of friends have limits to what they will endure, and she had unwittingly smacked right into one of Albert's limits as if it were an invisible brick wall.

Albert pushed up his glasses.

"I'd like to believe you," he said slowly, as if the thought was being formed before her very eyes. And it was, because who really knows if they believe in genies until the moment comes when you are asked to believe in them?

"If you'd like to, then do."

"It's not unusual for intellectually high-achieving socially awkward boys to believe in magical constructs, but I . . . I definitely need more information."

"Information? What do you want? Her tax return? Vital statistics?"

"I don't know. Something . . . tangible."

"You want to meet her?"

"That would help."

"Okay." Janna crossed her arms and nodded her head. "I wish my genie here, now. Poof!"

Eugenie stumbled hard against Albert as she appeared beside him.

"You might have a little consideration, dear," she said testily as she picked up her cane, then stood and adjusted her hat. "Good thing I was dressed to go out."

"Eugenie, this is Albert. Albert, this is Eugenie."

"How do you do?"

"Very well, thank you."

"So, I told Albert who you were."

"Yes. I am Janna's great-aunt on her father's side, twice removed. Her favorite great-aunt, I might add."

Albert looked at Eugenie a little doubtfully.

"Um—I told him the truth," Janna said.

"Oh. Okay." The three of them stood, looking at one another.

Albert peered in closely at Eugenie's face. "How old are you?"

"Albert!" Janna said.

"That's all right, dear. I'm several thousand years old, give or take a century."

"Forgot your birth date along with your name?" Janna asked.

Albert nodded at Eugenie. "I've done that before."

Eugenie looked at Janna in smug satisfaction.

"So, do something!" Janna said.

Eugenie looked at her and folded her arms. "*You* do something. You're the Queen of Poof."

"Albert, what do you want?"

Albert looked panicked. "I . . . want to fly?"

"Eugenie, I wish for Albert to be able to fly," Janna commanded, deepening her voice for dramatic effect.

"All-righty, then." Eugenie looked at Albert.

Albert looked around. "I can fly now?"

"Sure. Always could."

Janna stepped back as Albert flapped his arms tentatively.

"What do I need to do?"

"Go to jetblue.com. I've done it myself. Very user-friendly," Eugenie said. "And I love those chips." She cackled. Albert looked crushed.

"That was mean!" Janna said. "He meant really fly."

"Their planes don't pretend. That would be problematic."

"Oh, stop it. This is just for demonstration purposes. I wish for you to give him a pastrami on rye, no mustard. Poof."

A sandwich appeared in Albert's hand and he fumbled

it. He stared at it, then looked at Janna. "You know I always get pastrami on rye. So statistically that would have been a very safe thing to have waiting in the wings."

Janna sighed. "You're both morons. I'll choose. I've always wanted to meet Pit Bullard."

"The actor? Why?" Albert looked puzzled.

"He's . . . cute. Eugenie, I wish for you to take us to see Pit Bullard."

Janna felt a lurch in her stomach and then found herself in a strange room, where the walls were covered with mirrors and movie posters. At one end of the room the man in the movie posters was making faces at himself in a mirror. First there was the soulful, anguished looked he used often in *Love Possibly*, Janna's favorite. She sighed, and Albert gave her a revolted look. Then Bullard put on a pair of glasses and a fedora hat. He adjusted it several times, and when it was finally to his liking, he struck the pose he'd made famous as the tragic, handsome professor in *The Chemistry of Love*. It was a simultaneously scholarly and vulnerable expression proven to melt eight out of ten teenage girl hearts. Janna nearly drooled. After a few moments he took off the glasses and practiced raising one eyebrow. It didn't come naturally to him and he had to use his fingers—one to hold the eyebrow of his right eye up and one to pull the eyebrow of his left eye down. He tired of this and then turned around with his back to the mirror. Turning his head over one shoulder to view his reflection, he made a look of distaste and patted the pants down over his rump in a typical *Does this make my butt look big?* gesture. Albert snickered, and Bullard whirled around with a shriek.

"Who are you? Get out! Security! Help!"

"Mr. Bullard! Pit!" Janna stepped forward, extending her right hand. "What an honor! I'm such a fan of yours—"

"Not another step. Oh, God, you're one of those crazy types! Get away from me!" He screamed like a girl, permanently messing up Janna's image of him.

Janna stepped back, hands up. "Hey, you're shorter than you look on screen."

Pit Bullard lurched toward a button on the wall, and they heard a siren go off, followed by heavy steps on the stairs and dogs barking. The door was thrown open and two Doberman pinschers on leashes appeared, dragging a large man behind them.

"Get us out!" Janna yelled.

Eugenie just looked at her with a panicked face.

"What are you waiting for?" Janna shrieked.

"Wish it!" Albert yelled. "You have to wish it!"

"I wish for you to get us all out of here right now!"

As the man dropped the leashes and the dogs leapt, there was a *poof* and the three of them, plus the dogs, the security guard, and Pit Bullard all landed on the sidewalk in Janna's neighborhood with an assortment of oofs, whumps, and whines.

The dogs recovered more quickly than the humans and crouched to leap again.

"Not the dogs!" Janna cried. "Put them back! I mean, I wish the dogs weren't here!"

The dogs disappeared, leaving Pit Bullard and the security guard staring at two leashes attached to empty collars on the ground.

"Would you like to . . . come to my house and have some hot chocolate?" Janna suggested in the awkward silence that followed. She could just imagine trying to explain that to her mother.

Wide-eyed and stunned, Pit Bullard shook his head silently.

Janna sighed. "Okay. Sorry about all this. Maybe another time. Eugenie, I wish them back in Pit Bullard's house."

The men disappeared.

"Maybe if you had called first?" Eugenie said.

"*Maybe* if your sense of timing was a little better!" Janna said. "You can't just burst into someone's . . . whatever that room was!"

"I know that, but you're the one calling the shots!"

Janna sighed and turned to Albert, who was looking a little glassy-eyed.

"Statistically, what do you think of that?"

"That was definitely way out in the tail end someplace," Albert said, adjusting his glasses and taking a bite out of his sandwich.

"So you're on board with the genie thing?"

"Yup," Albert said. "I'm with you."

"So I cheated, but I didn't mean to, okay?

"You could have uncheated."

Janna was silent.

"Okay. Don't do it again. And you'll take another test that I make up."

"Deal." They tapped knuckles to seal it.

Albert turned back to Eugenie. "I have some questions, now that your veracity has been established."

"I can't cause emotions, no blanket wishes, no cash gifts in excess of twelve thousand dollars, and, yes, we do require a signed waiver," Eugenie rattled off.

"No. I want to know how come nobody just wishes for no limits on the number of wishes."

"There are no limits on the number of wishes."

"But—"

"Three has always been an artificial device to create tension in a story line," Janna and Eugenie recited together.

Albert stroked his chin. "And how come nobody wishes to have genie powers themselves?"

"Been done. Not advisable—the downside far outweighs the up," Eugenie said. She held her arms out. "Do I look like I'm cleaning up in this gig?

"There are other things that are possible, but also not advisable—like stopping the tides. The repercussions are—perhaps not universal but, shall we say, widespread? And what good really comes of it? Parting the Red Sea is about as far as I ever messed with natural forces."

"Okay. So how come nobody just wishes to have control of all the genies that exist?"

"Excellent question." Eugenie pondered a moment. "I'm pretty sure that is covered in Article 678 regarding monopolies, but I'll have to get back to you on that."

Albert looked disappointed, and Janna felt vaguely embarrassed that her apparently low-quality genie could be stumped so easily.

"Last question, at least for now. How do you handle illogical requests?"

"Illogical? I'm not sure I get your drift. Stupid, cruel, ridiculous, frivolous, vain, tacky, ostentatious, selfish, creepy, bizarre, vulgar—I've had to fulfill all those kinds of wishes, but what would be an illogical wish?"

"Well, what if I, a never-been-married male, wished I were a single girl again?"

Janna furrowed her brow at Albert. Eugenie stared at him.

"You are one strange child. You know that?"

"Sticks and stones," Albert said, holding his hands out for a few snowflakes that were starting to fall.

They heard the low belch of a conch shell being blown.

"That's my dad," Albert said to Eugenie, reading the look on her face. "I need to go now."

"We're done," Janna said. "I just . . . wanted you to understand."

Albert nodded, staring at the snowflakes. He held his hand out to catch a few.

"I have an idea," he said. "It's supposed to snow a ton tonight. What if we go around to the neighbors in the morning and offer to shovel them out?"

Janna looked at him as if he had grown three heads.

"I don't do shoveling."

"No! *She'll* do the shoveling," Albert pointed to Eugenie.

"I most certainly will not!" Eugenie said.

"Not real shoveling! *Poof* shoveling!" Albert said.

"Oh," Janna said. "But why?"

"It's a win-win. They get their snow gone—I'll bet Eugenie does a better job than we would—and we get to split the money three ways."

"Why?" Janna said.

Albert pointed to Eugenie. "One."

He pointed to Janna. "Two."

"Three." He pointed to himself.

"No, I mean what do you want the money for?"

"I'm saving for a new video card."

"Why don't I just poof you a new card?"

Albert pursed his lips. "That wouldn't feel quite . . . right."

Janna sighed. "You're not normal."

"Thank you," Albert said.

"Okay, we'll meet here at six thirty in the morning and see what business we can drum up."

Janna had no interest in this type of win-win, but after their uncomfortable spat she was willing to humor Albert.

The conch shell blew again.

"What a sweet boy," Eugenie said as they watched Albert walk back to his house.

Chapter 10

The next morning ten inches of white velvet blanketed the neighborhood. The three huddled and stamped on the corner in front of Janna's house trying to keep warm, waiting for the snowplow to come by.

"I could be sleeping in!" Janna fumed. "They canceled school because of all this white stuff. And the temperature is dropping."

Albert and Eugenie ignored her, peering at a clipboard Albert held in his gloved hand. "Everybody on the north side signed up for Al-Jan's Super Snow Removal Service."

"Only four on the south side signed up for Jan-Bert's," Janna said. "What did you say to get all of them to sign up?"

"I promised it done five minutes after the snowplow came by or double their money back."

"Did anyone point out that you weren't carrying a snow shovel?"

"With a guarantee like that, they don't care how we do it. We could be carrying flamethrowers and they wouldn't bat an eye."

"Agreed. But you weren't carrying *anything*."

They heard the grumble of the snowplow the next block over. Albert pulled his coat sleeve up to see his watch.

"T minus five, everyone. Synchronize." He looked at Eugenie. "You can do this, right?"

"In my sleep, child, in my sleep," Eugenie replied. "But Janna's right. It is way too cold to be out here, so let's get this over with. Even with my charming new headgear, my ears feel like ice cubes and my lips are officially numb."

The snowplow approached the first house on the block. Huge piles of snow were pushed in front and to the side, leaving a dense, chunky three-foot mountain blocking the end of the Kramers' driveway.

"Wait for it . . . ," Albert said. "Now!"

"I wish for the snow at the Kramers' to disappear," Janna said, and, just for fun, she clapped her hands.

The snow mountain disappeared, as well as every flake on the lawn. They got a glimpse of Mrs. Kramer looking out the window, a strange look on her face.

"Don't be so literal!" Janna said. "I wish for you to put

back the snow except for what was on the concrete."

Once again the lawn was blanketed white. The concrete was not only clear of snow, it was bone-dry. The look on Mrs. Kramer's face got stranger. Then she disappeared.

"That is certifiably awesome," Albert said as they walked across to collect their money, handed to them by a silent, startled Mrs. Kramer.

Twenty minutes later they walked back to Janna's house, their pockets full of cash and checks.

"Hey!" Janna said, stopping and staring at her house, which was surrounded by what had to be twelve times more snow than the neighbors' houses, rising to above the top of the windows on the first story. Good thing her mom had already gotten Maybe out of the driveway to go to work.

"That is so not funny!"

"That is so righteous!" Albert said, and ran full tilt to jump into the mountain of snow.

"Get rid of it!" Janna said, between her teeth.

"And where do you suggest I put it?"

"The desert, outer space, the ocean, how should I know?" Janna said. "I don't care. Away."

Eugenie just looked at her stubbornly.

"I wish you to remove this extra snow, and you can't put it back where it came from."

"I keep telling you, there *is* no 'away,'" Eugenie grumbled, but Albert was left on his face when the mountain of snow vanished.

They stomped off the snow and took off their jackets in the hallway.

"I am so cold that I will never get warm. Let's have something hot," Janna said, heading for the kitchen.

Albert spread his collected fees on the kitchen table and began to divide it into two piles, one for cash and one for checks. Janna dug into her pockets and added her contributions. Albert picked out one of the checks she'd laid down.

"You didn't let Mr. Hester give you a check, did you?"

"He said he didn't have the cash," Janna said.

"Never take a check from Mr. Hester. Ever," Albert said. "This is worthless."

"Are you sure?"

Eugenie reached across and touched the check.

"Yup. Worthless."

"Then, I wish he gets his snow back, plus a few inches," Janna said. "Poof."

"I'm down with that," Eugenie said. "Maybe we could officially make Mr. Hester 'away.'"

Albert grinned and got up to check it out.

"What's wrong with this picture?" Janna asked him when he returned to the kitchen.

He squinted at her, then shook his head.

"Note the goose bumps." She pointed to her arm. She pointed to her mug. "Note the hot chocolate."

"It's supposed to be cold. It's winter. Given the concern about global warming, we should be grateful."

"But I hate being cold. And it occurs to me that I don't need to stay where it's cold."

"I get your drift," Eugenie said. "Caribbean? South Seas? Seychelles?"

"We don't want to just lounge around. What we want is a destination location," Janna said. "Someplace that has it all. Someplace with rides, food, sun, and fun. Someplace like . . . Disney World!"

"I'm not so—," Albert started to say, but Janna interrupted him.

"Eugenie, I wish you to take us to Disney World!"

They were instantly elsewhere, on a shuttle bus someplace chock-full of people dressed in loud warm-weather clothing and sunglasses. And there they were, right in the middle, wearing their sweaters and long pants, their cheeks red from the cold. Janna was still cradling her mug of hot chocolate.

"Psst," Janna said to Eugenie, and whispered into her ear. They became clothed in shorts, sandals, and T-shirts. Albert's T-shirt said I'M WITH STUPID. Albert eyed it doubtfully, then looked at Janna's, which said IT'S ALL ABOUT ME. Eugenie was clad in clingy leopard-skin leggings and a slinky white shirt. She was carrying a matching leopard-skin bag and wearing a floppy sun hat with a matching leopard-print band. Gold earrings jangled from her ears;

gold bangles clattered on her wrists. Her black galoshes had been replaced by three-inch black heels, but she grimaced and wiggled her feet, and the heels were replaced by high-top sneakers. Albert stared. Janna rolled her eyes.

"Now, remember, kids," the moon-faced man next to them instructed his children, a boy dressed all in camouflage, and a girl in various glittery stretchy items of clothing. "Get those pointy little elbows out to the side and don't be afraid to use them! Ribs and stomachs are especially vulnerable. Got it?"

The two kids squared off, elbows forming little triangular weapons at their sides, gleams in their eyes, their mouths set in competitive pouts.

"Isn't there enough fun for everyone?" Eugenie asked him. He narrowed his eyes at her.

"It's a vicious world out there from the day you're born, lady. I'm giving them lessons they can use all their lives."

When the shuttle stopped, Janna, Albert, and Eugenie descended the stairs, jostled and nearly trampled by a multicolored horde. Mr. Pointy Elbows and his progeny were, of course, the first ones off, but the man's backpack straps became entangled somehow with the shuttle door hinge.

"Help me!" he squeaked at his son and daughter. They left the family there, the children trying to free their father, who was twisting and turning in vain.

Albert smiled at Eugenie.

"How long are they going to be tied up?"

"Only until everyone gets a good head start."

"When they do sort themselves out, is it possible that they could find themselves in very long lines?"

"It could happen," Eugenie said.

"Speaking of lines," Janna said. "Can we always be first?"

"That's piggy," Albert said. "How about if we're always about ninth or tenth in line, with the tiredest and littlest kids before us?"

Eugenie looked at Janna, who rolled her eyes. Eugenie still looked at her.

"Oh, okay. Poof—I wish it so. But how are we going to pay for all of this?"

Eugenie shrugged. "I think a pass is easiest. Something we can charge everything to."

"A PoofPass!" Janna said.

"I've never heard of one of those," Albert said.

"There will only ever be three of them," Janna said. "Eugenie, I wish for a PoofPass for each of us."

A shiny golden ticket appeared in each of their hands.

When they walked toward the front of the line and waved the PoofPasses, the crowds parted. In fact, every line they approached for the next few hours fell back after precisely the tenth person to let them in. And people *smiled* at them when they cut the line.

As they waited for the super-free-fall roller coaster, the little girl behind them whined, "Mommy, I'm tired. Can we just sit down?"

"You can't afford to be tired. Do you know how much this costs?"

"I'm not sure I understand the goal here," Eugenie said.

"Well, that's not it," Albert said. "Make that mother sleep the rest of the afternoon." Janna nodded and wished it, and the woman began snoring on her feet. With relief the little girl walked over to a tree and curled up on the grass.

As the family ahead of them advanced, the little boy began to fret.

"Daddy, I don't want to go on that ride! It's too scary!" The little boy's chin quivered.

"You will go on it, and you will like it, young man! We did not come all this way for you to be a big baby."

Albert got an alarmed look on his face, and Janna knew he was screwing up his courage to talk to the father. She put her hand on Albert's arm to stop him.

"Eugenie, I wish for that little boy to discover that he loves free fall," Janna whispered. "And for his father to be so scared on that ride that he wets his pants."

Chapter 11

Six hours later every ride had been ridden—many of them more than once—all of the food stands had been visited, and the PoofPasses were looking a little tarnished.

"I think I had too much fun," Albert said, with a hand on his belly.

"Me too," Janna said, looking as if she'd eaten worms.

"More! More! More!" Eugenie whacked them both with her cane.

"I can't," Albert groaned. "No. More. Roller. Coasters."

"No. More. Sugar," Janna said. "I think I need a chiropractor."

"Weaklings!" Eugenie said, whacking again.

"Hey, stop it! Just because you look like a demented old lady doesn't mean you get to act like one!"

"Where's the fun in that? Come on! The lion feeding is in ten minutes."

"Can I ask you something?" Janna said.

"You just did."

"Why do you have that cane, when you obviously don't need it to get around?"

Eugenie bent her knees and struck a pose, hands held above her head, the cane between them.

"Protection."

"Of course."

"Let's just go lie on a beach for a little while," Albert said. "Soak up the sun, listen to the surf."

"That sounds good to me," Janna said.

"What? You haven't even been to the gift shops!" Eugenie said. "That's not the Janna I know."

Janna shook her head. "I . . . just want to rest. Albert's right. I wish for us to be at a nice, calm, quiet beach."

"Poof," Eugenie said, and they lay on an empty white sand beach, a gentle surf lapping a few feet away. Janna looked at their shirts and shorts.

"I wish we had swimsuits!" she commanded, then shrieked. "Not a bikini!"

"And I don't do Speedos!" Albert yelled.

"Youth is truly wasted upon the young," Eugenie said. She snapped her fingers, clothing them in less revealing attire. For herself she chose a bright purple and gold lamé swim-dress, fire-engine-red lips and nails, and a large brimmed hat with several pieces of fruit attached.

"I do not believe you," Janna said.

"Maybe you should put your coat back on," Albert said.

"One of the advantages of being a couple of millennia old is that I am finally comfortable in my own skin," Eugenie replied, leaning back and putting on an extremely large pair of sunglasses.

Eugenie snapped her fingers, and a man appeared in waiter's attire, right down to a little bow tie. He sauntered up to them slowly, a tray in one hand, a towel draped over his arm.

"Where did *he* spring from?" Albert said.

"Yes, miss?" He bowed respectfully in front of Janna.

"Lemonade, please," Janna said.

The waiter held his bow. Janna looked sideways at Eugenie.

"Wish it!" Eugenie mouthed.

Janna cleared her throat. "I wish for three lemonades. Fresh squeezed in fancy glasses with those little umbrellas in them."

"Mademoiselle has excellent taste." He gave a moue and then strutted away, a little stiff-legged.

"Why does he walk like that?" Janna asked.

"Did you, like . . . do something to him?" Albert asked. "He doesn't look . . . quite normal."

"Normal is relative, and we are in Florida," Eugenie said. "But . . . I did tweak him just a little."

"Wasn't his nose . . . like, really huge?" Janna said.

"And where is he going to get our drinks? There's no place around here," Albert said.

Nonetheless, the waiter appeared again a short distance away, walking with his chest puffed forward.

"Caw," he said as he handed them their drinks. Albert and Janna looked at each other. The waiter cleared his throat and tried again.

"Is there anything else mademoiselle would like?"

"No, thank you. We're all set here," Janna said.

They settled in with their drinks and watched the sun on the slow waves.

"I have a question for you, flyboy," Eugenie said, and turned to Albert. "If you had me in your power, what would you wish for? Not, of course, that ownership of me is transferable."

"Give it up," Janna said. "I've already asked him. Nothing but computers on the brain."

"That was before I knew you were talking about wishes that . . . could bend the rules a bit. That changes things," Albert said. "That opens up all sorts of possibilities."

"Like?" Eugenie said.

"I want to know: Is time an arrow, a river, or a whirlpool?" Albert asked.

"What?" Eugenie looked blank.

"And is there intelligent life elsewhere in the universe?"

"Wait a minute," Eugenie said, holding her free hand up.

"Are quarks and leptons fundamental, or are there even smaller bits of matter?"

"Stop it!" Eugenie yelled.

Albert fell silent and pushed his glasses up.

"Do I look like Einstein?" Eugenie jammed her fingers into her hair.

"When you do that, yes," Albert said.

"Well, I'm not even related, okay? I don't do physics, or know any more about cosmology than you'll learn in a good college. I grant wishes. I don't know how I do what I do, and I really don't care, okay? A talent for languages runs in some families. Granting wishes runs in mine."

Albert nodded in understanding. "Then, I guess I'd like to travel back to when the pyramids were built to see how they were constructed."

Eugenie shook her head. "They've cracked down ever since the time terrorists. The visa application requires an extensive background check and a psychiatric exam. Takes a lifetime. Literally."

"Couldn't I even . . . just see real dinosaurs for a few minutes?"

"Sorry, buddy," Eugenie said. "We've had writers who've taken liberties with that kind of stuff. Gotta be careful."

Albert looked crestfallen.

"Surely you have some other wish that doesn't wrinkle time or the fabric of the universe?"

"Well, I'd like to be a rock star guitarist . . . "

Janna stared at Albert. He blushed.

" . . . or a famous scientist. You know, all those unsolved theorems, maybe even a Nobel Prize." Albert glanced up, appealingly.

Eugenie smiled. "Big dreams for a boy. A bit beyond Elizabeth Newby's wardrobe." She glanced at Janna. Janna looked away.

"You seem a bright, responsible young man. At least the term 'big picture' seems to be in your vocabulary. . . . How would you change the world?"

"When did this shift from what he wanted to changing the world?" Janna asked.

"Why can't it be the same thing?" Eugenie responded, sticking her chin out.

Albert looked unsure, an uncommon occurrence in Janna's experience.

"My dad says the only way to change the world is to do the right thing."

"But there are a lot of people who do that already, aren't there?" Janna said.

"Well, there are little right things, and then there are big right things," Eugenie said. "And doing the right thing all the time, when you're tired or scared or know nobody's watching, that's really hard."

"My dad says that if everyone did the right thing most of the time, things would be different," Albert said, then paused. "But what I don't understand is—how do you know what the right thing is?"

"Isn't that always the question?" Eugenie said, staring at the ocean.

"I wish I could stay here forever," Janna said, and sighed, wriggling her toes in the hot sand.

Albert and Eugenie turned to look at her.

"Not really wish, just *wish* wish," Janna corrected. They sat in silence, lost in thought until Janna stretched, looked at her watch, and groaned.

"Time to go. My mom will be home in half an hour. I wish for our winter clothing back. Well, I don't, but you know what I mean. Poof."

They gathered up their hats and coats and started putting them on in the hot sun.

"Ouch!" Albert said.

"Right," Janna said, wincing as well. "Eugenie, I wish you would poof these sunburns, okay?"

She took a last look around and sighed. "Can you wish for something in the distant future?"

"Theoretically, yes," Eugenie said. "Although I've never hung around to verify the results."

"I wish that someday I live someplace sunny and warm by the ocean."

They looked at one another, but of course nothing happened.

"I wish you to take us back to my house," Janna said, less than eagerly.

As they left, Janna could have sworn she saw a seagull sporting a bow tie strutting on the beach.

Chapter 12

Janna looked at herself with satisfaction. No, it was more than satisfaction—it was delight, it was approval, it would have been envy had she been looking at someone else. She had on a new sweater, new jeans, and new certifiably awesome boots. Okay, so Elizabeth Newby's clothes were not to be had, but Janna had realized that it wasn't Elizabeth Newby's clothes that she wanted. What she wanted was to look as stunning as Elizabeth Newby did, while still looking like Janna Danner. If she had shown up in class in a strappy floral pattern dress, pointy-toed shoes, and fake diamonds, people would have wondered who she was and what she had done with the real Janna Danner. Well, now she'd gotten it right.

The softest cashmere sweater in a shade of teal that made her eyes gleam; the skinniest, coolest jeans she had ever even *seen*; and a pair of leather boots that made the rest of the outfit absolutely rock. She had spent a fair amount of time the night before pointing out examples on the Web and in catalogs. Eugenie had observed that the jeans didn't look new—in fact, were a little tattered, but when Janna explained that was how they were *supposed* to look, Eugenie had just rolled her eyes and given in. And there, in the morning, was her dream outfit. Janna had gone down to breakfast in her regular old clothes, but once her mother had kissed her good-bye, she'd bolted back upstairs to change. Eugenie hadn't tried any tricks, and everything fit as if handmade for her. She looked good, she felt great, if she had been a cat, she would have purred. *Move aside, Elizabeth Newby, make way for* me.

Reluctantly, Janna put her thrift store coat on. She had totally forgotten to specify a new coat. Shame to cover up such nice duds; like wrapping a gleaming jewel in burlap. As she walked to the bus stop, she was conscious at every step of how her feet felt inside the thick new leather boots that clopped so thrillingly on the sidewalk, and of how positively luxurious the sweater felt on her skin.

Janna stepped onto the bus feeling so obviously a new person that she was a little disappointed that a hush didn't settle as everyone turned their eyes toward her apprais-ingly. In fact, nobody turned to look at her at all. Like always, they were involved in their pocket games, books, and music. The same few kids she always said hi to said hi back, but that was it. Well, she did still have the coat on. Just wait until she got to school. She sat down next to Albert, who gave his customary eyebrow raise in greeting and then went back to his book. She knew better than to try to get Albert to notice her wardrobe.

At her locker she hung her coat up and brushed her hair. There. She knew she looked like a million bucks, and she felt like two million. She stepped into the hallway and looked for a reaction. The mill and buzz surrounded her and she searched for people she knew.

"Hi," Janna said, falling into step with Pat Hundley, who had first period Spanish with her.

"Hi." Pat was always friendly.

"My feet are killing me," Janna said. "New boots take so long to break in."

Pat nodded in sympathy. "I still have a blister from mine."

Janna stopped and leaned against the wall to fake-adjust her boot. Pat stopped obligingly but didn't seem that interested in Janna's footwear.

"I have some Band-Aids in my backpack if you need them," was all Pat said.

Janna gave up, and they walked down the hall. She watched the faces in the oncoming traffic, ready to flash a bright smile at anyone who seemed to register the amazing clothes she was wearing. A few people looked at her quizzically when they saw her watching them, but a hesitant smile was all she elicited from them.

Nonetheless, Janna felt her own presence in a way she never had before. She felt confident; she felt . . . proud to be herself. She hadn't understood the phrase "walking tall" until now. In Spanish she raised her hand more than usual, and Ms. Luna clearly noticed. So did all the other kids, but nobody said *Wow, nice sweater!* Or *Where did you get those fantastic jeans?*

She tried again on her way to second period science. She saw Elizabeth Newby in a cluster of kids and, taking a breath, walked up to her. If anyone would notice what she had on, it would be Elizabeth Newby.

"Hi," she said to Elizabeth. They weren't friends. They knew each other, but invisible boundaries had been firmly in place, until now.

"Hi," Elizabeth said. Everyone stopped talking to look at Janna.

"Quite the excitement at your house the other night," Janna said. "I . . . just wanted to see if everything was okay."

Elizabeth furrowed her brow, and Janna understood too late that perhaps it wasn't a comfortable topic for her. "It was so weird. My mom really flipped out. But, yeah, everything's cool."

Janna nodded. She wasn't sure what she'd expected, but Elizabeth hadn't even assessed Janna's attire.

"Thanks for asking," Elizabeth said, staring at Janna.

Janna nodded, turned on the heel of her brand-new

boot, and walked away, feeling the other kids' eyes on her.

In lab she was paired with Glen Kruse, a big intimidating jock; very cute, but not so smart. All the girls wanted to be his partner, but the last time Janna had been stuck with him, they'd gotten a "do over" on the assignment. Faced with those gorgeous brown eyes and white, white teeth, she'd been a little reluctant to point out the step that he'd skipped in the protocol, and as a result, their experiment had bombed, fortunately not literally. This time Janna was unwilling to be dragged down, and somehow the teal sweater and boots gave her the courage to say, "Wait! It doesn't say fifty milliliters, it says five milliliters."

Glen looked at her with surprise, reread the lab sheet, and then said, "Oh, good catch. You think it might make a difference?"

They continued, and twenty minutes later Glen looked at her with respect. "Wow, it worked! That's the first time I've had an experiment go right! I want to be lab rats with you every time!"

Three girls in the class glared at her as she walked out to history class.

By lunch Janna was desperate. She grabbed Gail Goldstein outside the cafeteria and dragged her into the girl's rest room. Their kindergarten altercation long forgotten, she knew she could count on Gail for both good taste and discretion.

Once inside, she pirouetted before Gail like a ballerina.

"Notice anything?"

Gail stepped forward. "Yeah, you've got this glob of fuzz in your hair." She reached up and removed it. "There you go. All better."

"Fuzz," Janna said. "That's it? What about my new sweater?"

Gail looked stricken. "I am *so* sorry. That is *such* a nice color on you, Janna! I really, really like it!"

"And my new boots?"

Having belatedly gushed over the sweater, Gail realized she couldn't do the same over the boots and sound sincere. "They're nice too, but it's the sweater that really brings out your eyes."

Janna sighed. Gail knew what was cool, and if she hadn't noticed, nobody would. How was it she felt different, even acted a little different, but the clothes apparently didn't matter to anyone else?

"Thanks," she said to Gail. "Let's go eat."

It made Janna glum to realize that nice things were nice to have but that in the final analysis that was about all they were good for. They didn't change your day that much. But if things wouldn't make a difference in her life, what would?

"So how did it go?" Eugenie asked when Janna had gotten home and clumped upstairs in her dream outfit.

"Nobody noticed anything! It was as if I was . . . plain old me!"

"It's all any of us ever will be, Janna," Eugenie said, smiling. "The trick is for plain old you to be awesome—just like me."

Janna didn't smile, but flung herself down onto her bed. Who knew being happy was so hard? By far what she had enjoyed most since Eugenie's arrival was their day of warmth at the amusement park and beach. What else did she want that wasn't a *thing*?

Janna had always wanted to play the piano, but it didn't come easily to her. She never got the rhythm right, no matter how many times Mrs. Lathrop would say patiently, *Tap it out. Listen to it. Again. Again.* The sounds Janna ended up making were so at odds with the ones she wanted to make that she quit in frustration after several months of lessons. The keyboard she had begged her mother for lived under her bed now, amidst the lost socks and stuff she didn't want to take time to put away.

Still, Janna loved the tuxedo look of the black and white keys, loved the feeling of sitting down with her hands poised above the piano, ready to unleash . . . in her case, a cacophony. She felt like she had beautiful music in her. So why couldn't it come out through her fingers? Well, now it could. One wish to Eugenie and she, Janna, could be an even better piano player than she would have been had she practiced ten times as much as Mrs. Lathrop had suggested.

Janna sat up. "Eugenie, I wish to play the piano. Not just play it—play it beautifully."

Eugenie cocked her head. "Now, that's the first thing you've wished for that I even remotely understand wanting. So be it."

Janna looked at her hands, which didn't look any different but felt a little prickly all of a sudden, as if they were itching to get at the keyboard.

Janna pulled her keyboard out from under the bed and placed it on its stand. Too bad it had only sixty-one keys, but she could wish for a baby grand once she figured out where to put it. She sat on the piano stool and raised her hands above the keys. Then, suddenly shy, she stopped.

"Go away," she said to Eugenie. Eugenie looked disappointed. "Please? It's . . . private."

"Okay," Eugenie grumbled, but she disappeared.

Janna brought her fingers down to the keys slowly, apprehensively. She needn't have worried; her hands were happy to be there. The soft chord they produced caused Janna to smile, and a small thrill ran through her. Her hands rose again and her fingers spread out farther than she ever thought they could have, and came down again, harder. This time the chord was louder, deeper, and even more thrilling. *Oh, my*, Janna thought. *Oh, my.*

After that, Janna gave up trying to exert any control over

her hands. She didn't need to—even though she hadn't put any sheet music on the tray, it didn't matter—her fingers knew their way up the keyboard and down, over each other, crossed at the wrists, and back again. The music was something vaguely familiar, a rising crescendo here, a soft adagio there. She closed her eyes and let her body follow where her hands took it. When she opened her eyes, there were her hands still at it, ten little digits taking instruction not from her brain or heart but from . . . something else. It was beautiful music. It was amazing to sit there and watch her hands, *her hands*, be the ones to elicit it, but in the midst of it all Janna felt detached. Her hands got a workout, and Janna began to wonder when they were going to stop, because she'd tried to stop playing and couldn't. She was getting a little bored, actually, and her fingers were starting to tire. She could hear the piece winding down, though, and indeed, her hands were dancing more slowly now. When the piece was over, Janna sat at the keyboard, her face a little sweaty from the exertion, her hands aching with the unfamiliar exercise. She sat there until she noticed that Eugenie had reappeared.

"That was lovely, dear," Eugenie said, then stopped at the look on Janna's face. "What's the matter? Not professional-sounding enough for you?"

"I felt . . . like a robot."

"Well, that's sort of what you were."

"But I wanted to be able to do it myself."

"If you could do it yourself, you wouldn't need me. You know how to get to Carnegie Hall, right?"

At Janna's blank look Eugenie added, "Practice, practice, practice."

Janna sighed.

Chapter 13

The next day after school Janna stood in front of her mirror trying on different outfits. She sighed and turned to pull another color off a four-foot stack of sweaters. Having stuff was so . . . tiring. And space was really becoming an issue. She understood now why Elizabeth Newby's room was such a mess.

To top it off, Eugenie kept forgetting—Janna suspected on purpose—to make things invisible when Janna's mother was home. She picked up her pile of rejected clothes and tossed them at Eugenie, who was on the top bunk reading a book called *The Fundamentals of Wealth Redistribution.*

"Get rid of these," she said. "I mean, I wish you would please get rid of these."

"Poof," Eugenie replied, not looking up, and the clothes were gone.

"I need to figure out a way to get my mom to add on to the house. Maybe she could get a letter in the mail that preapproved her for an interest-free loan with no payments for ninety-nine years?"

"I don't think you'll need to. At the rate you're going I'll only be here a week or so more."

"*What* did you say?"

Eugenie looked up. "Each master gets a thousand genie watts, and you're using yours up big-time, especially with all this poof-unpoof, visible-invisible stuff."

"Genie watts! Like energy? But you said there was no limit on the number of my wishes!" Janna said.

"There isn't a limit on the number. Some wishes take a lot of genie watts; some don't take so much. You can make a million wishes if you want, or maybe only one or two really big hunkers, depending on what you wish for."

"You never told me that!" Janna yelled. "You're trying to cheat me! I haven't even *begun* to get this wishing thing right, and you're telling me I'm almost done? I'm . . . I'm going to register a complaint! There distinctly has not been full disclosure here!"

"Calm down. You're getting the same deal everyone else gets. How could I cheat you?"

Janna turned back to the window and stared out across to Elizabeth's room. Elizabeth had it all without having to cope with this genie nonsense. It wasn't fair.

"I don't understand." Janna sighed. "You're here to grant my wishes, but my wishes aren't working out right. Are you sure you're qualified? Don't they give you guys any training in customer service? Like—the customer is always right?"

"You and I know that is a load of malarkey. Reasonable people know they are not always right."

"I can't help but think you're making things difficult on purpose. You don't tell me the most important rule about having a genie, and you say you can't make things happen on your own, but you do! I saw what you did to that seagull on the beach!"

"Stray voltage."

"You turned a seagull into a cabana boy with stray voltage?"

Eugenie nodded.

"All I want is to be happy."

"Every master I have ever had has wanted to be happy. And every master I have ever had has tried to get there by asking me for things. And none of my masters has ended up happy. Things. Don't. Make. You. Happy."

"This isn't fair!"

"Janna, I'm going to tell you something. Extra special deal, just for you, so listen up. There are two things you might as well save your breath on, because everyone automatically stops listening to you the second they hear them. The first is *'It's not fair'* and the second is *'It's not my fault.'*"

Janna turned away to hide the tears beginning to form in her eyes. Then she whirled to face the genie. "I wish you would just disappear!"

Instantly, the genie was gone.

"Come back!" Janna cried. "I didn't mean it! I wish you would come back!"

The genie immediately reappeared, on the top bunk.

Janna took a steadying breath. "So, precisely how many genie watts do I have left?"

Eugenie stared at Janna silently for a moment, chin in hand.

"I can't tell you that, but I will offer you a deal."

"I can't imagine that your kind of deal will work to my advantage."

"Just hear me out. If you don't use any genie watts for twenty-four hours, and if you will come with me tonight, I will let you start over with the full one thousand genie watts."

"Can you do that?"

"Well"—Eugenie didn't meet Janna's eyes—"I haven't turned in my accounting for the week. You have no idea how much paperwork your poof-unpoof thing is causing me! And with the International Date Line, I'm flying a little below Steve's radar right now."

"Steve? Who's Steve?"

"My manager. Head of my genie division."

"Division?"

Eugenie sighed. "They're always reorganizing us. This century it's divisions. At least it beats the 1500s when they were into matrix management. But the standardized testing they are trying to put in place is a disaster, and don't get me started on how they want to cut back on our benefits!"

"Benefits?"

"Such as stray voltage. We can accumulate them, so many watts per job. The idea is to keep us out there drumming up business. I was plumb out of watts when you found me at the thrift store. Imagine having all this power, yet not even being able to keep your own ears from freezing."

"Are all the genies in your . . . division . . . bag ladies?"

"Of course not. That was my own inspiration. We're organized by age and experience." Eugenie permitted herself a small, superior smile. "I'm quite high up on the career ladder."

Janna thought she would happily trade less experience for more docility but kept that to herself.

"Why is it so wrong to want things?" Janna asked.

"It's not," Eugenie said. "Everybody should have the basics. What's wrong is to believe that things make you *happy*. At Genie Research and Development, experiments have proven that possessions are addictive. The more you have, the more you want, on and on, forever, and you're never satisfied. That's why we enacted the genie watt restriction. Without it, some doofus would eventually ask for everything, and then where would the world be?"

Eugenie hopped nimbly from the top bunk and advanced eagerly toward Janna.

"I believe that people who try to fill up on things are really missing something else in their lives. It's as if they have a black hole in their heart and everything they acquire falls straight through that hole. They are left more miserable than before. And misery is infinitely contagious."

"But there are happy people in the world."

"Of course there are, but it's not their things that make them happy, and they know it."

"Yeah, yeah, yeah," Janna said, "the best things in life aren't things."

"In Australia, for instance, there is a tribe that believes that everything should be passed on. They think that if you keep something, it gets stuck and will bring you bad luck. Now, there's an advanced civilization!"

Eugenie came to stand in front of Janna and looked directly into her eyes.

"After a few millennia of helping the rich get richer and the poor get poorer, I guess I'm having a career crisis. I've spent eons watching adults who were convinced that the more they had, the better life would be, only to find out in the end it just ain't so. I'm thinking that the change has to begin with kids, kids like you. You can do better, Janna. I hate to be trite, since the one thing kids of your age cannot cope with is triteness, but you can change the world."

"I don't want to change the world!"

"Instead of wasting this opportunity on trinkets that will bore you tomorrow, or cheating on tests because you're too lazy to learn, you could make a difference. You have a chance to make the world a better place. Maybe in a small way, but still, what a chance!"

Janna was silent.

"What about all the children who will go to bed hungry tonight? Is that fair? Can't you find something in your heart for them?" Eugenie asked.

"It's not my fault," Janna said, pouting.

Eugenie merely looked at her.

"I can't change the world," Janna insisted.

"But you already have."

"What do you mean?"

"Everybody changes the world, just by being here.

Some change it for the better, some don't. It's your choice. Look what happened when you were kind to me. A simple hat and here we are."

"It's not like every old lady is a genie."

"You might be surprised." Eugenie grinned.

"So you think kindness can change the world?"

"Absolutely! Haven't you noticed that some days it seems that almost the entire world is grumpy? That's because almost the entire world *is* grumpy. You wake up and snarl at your mom, and your mom drives to work and yells at someone on the road who is driving *her* kids to school. So that mom yells at her kids, and they take it to school and spread it around faster than the flu, and in less than an hour the whole school has been infected by your nasty little snarl.

"Fortunately, not everybody succumbs to a grump epidemic every time it happens. It's like the flu: Sometimes you catch it, sometimes you don't. And like with most diseases, some people's immune systems are just better."

"What makes people immune to grumpiness?" Janna asked.

"Falling in love makes people unbelievably immune, but we don't yet understand the mechanics of that process. Good dreams help too, because dreams come from the soul, and happiness hides out there the longest. The morning after a good dream, you're happy, and so you act a little nicer. You don't argue when you usually would; you do your chores without complaining; maybe you share your lunch with someone who forgot theirs. The most reliable and effective antidote to grumpiness is deliberate kindness. Occasionally you get a truly exceptional person who simply decides to consciously counter every negative thing they experience with something positive, and you should see the effects of that!"

Janna considered for a moment. "Albert would call flying below Steve's radar dishonest."

"Yes, Albert would. But I'm going to call it cutting a few corners for the greater good. And you did show me two kindnesses, so that should count for something."

"Where are you going tonight?" Janna asked.

"No place you haven't been in the daylight. I'll even make us invisible if it would make you feel any better."

And when that didn't elicit a reply from Janna, Eugenie said, "You can bring Albert along if you'd like."

"Why would I want Albert along? I don't need two of you against me."

"Albert is a nice person," Eugenie said. "And it's a fact that there is greater safety in the presence of a kind soul."

Janna pondered. "My mom has another school board meeting tonight, so I can be gone for a while. But I need to be home by nine."

"Then you agree."

The thought of the additional genie watts made Janna itch. She was quite certain that nothing Eugenie could do would change her mind. And next time she wouldn't waste a single milliwatt. She would get it right.

Janna nodded. "I agree."

Chapter 14

"I will probably be late tonight, dear," Carol Danner said to Janna that night at dinner. "This is the last meeting before the vote tomorrow, and I'm sure it's not going to be pleasant. I understand that Mr. Pizer is going to have all of his buddies there."

Janna hadn't seen her mother look so worn-out for a long time. No sooner had Janna's mother left than Eugenie appeared standing by the kitchen table.

"Come on! Places to go. Things to see."

"Let's get this over with," Janna said, pulling on her coat. Secretly she was fine-tuning the wish list she had been working on over the last couple hours. By tomorrow, if all went well, she would have everything on that list safely in her possession, and Eugenie would be off her hands and out of her life for good. "I told Albert to walk over once he saw my mom leave, so he should be here right about"—*thud* tap tap tap—"now."

Albert opened the door, and Janna and Eugenie stared. He was dressed all in black, complete with balaclava and gloves.

"I'm feeling a little . . . underdressed," Eugenie said, surveying her worn multicolored garments.

"How did you explain this getup to your father?" Janna asked.

"*My* father?" Albert said. "Notice how someone was dressed?"

"Right. Okay, but lose the balaclava."

With a sigh Albert removed it.

Once out of Janna's house Eugenie proceeded purposefully across the street to the Newbys' house and marched straight up to the front door, which she opened without hesitation.

"Hey!" cried Albert. "It's customary to knock first!"

"They can't see us, can't hear us. I have made it so," reassured Eugenie, but Janna and Albert still looked at each other askance as they walked right into the Newbys'.

Eugenie clumped loudly into the center of the Newby living room. Janna and Albert tiptoed behind her, Albert sliding flat along the wall until Janna rolled her eyes at him.

"You're invisible, dork!" she hissed at him.

Albert slumped. He had been having fun.

Mr. Newby sat behind a newspaper, and Mrs. Newby

sat staring at the television, a glass of wine in her hand. Neither of them paid any attention to their visitors.

Elizabeth walked into the room. "I want a new dog!"

The Newbys' dog raised his head from the floor and cocked it. Neither Mr. Newby nor Mrs. Newby responded.

"I said," Elizabeth began more loudly, "*I want a new dog!*"

Mr. Newby rattled his newspaper, but did not put it down. Mrs. Newby clicked the remote and brought her wine glass to her lips.

"Listen to me!" shrieked Elizabeth.

Mr. Newby set his jaw and lowered his newspaper. "What's wrong with Barney? He's a perfectly good dog. You picked him out yourself."

"Well, now I don't want a mutt. I want a famous kind of dog. Like you see those actors carrying in little bags. And I want some little bags, too. Some that match my outfits and the dog's."

"Elizabeth, dear," her mother started timidly. "You can't just get rid of a dog."

"Of course you can!" Elizabeth yelled. "If you loved me, you would get me a new dog!"

"Barney loves us," her mother said. "We're supposed to love him."

"I will not get you a new dog, and that's final, young lady!" Mr. Newby yelled. He threw his paper down onto the floor and left the room, nearly running over Albert on his way out. Elizabeth stomped up the stairs. Mrs. Newby, who had not taken her eyes from the TV during this exchange, clicked the remote and poured herself another glass of wine. Janna thought she saw the reflection of tears in her eyes.

Janna and Albert followed Eugenie out of the house.

"What a spoiled brat!" Janna said.

Eugenie poked Janna in the shoulder. "Even at her worst I doubt that Elizabeth has demanded one of everything from a catalog."

"You did that?" Albert asked. "Where did you put it all?"

Janna scowled.

Eugenie took off at a good pace, and they had to trot to keep up with her. Janna had lived in the town all her life, but Eugenie knew the alleys and the back ways even better. Along the way Eugenie pointed out her favorite haunts and sleeping spots as if she were conducting a celebrity tour of Hollywood.

"If you know the schedules, you get the best pickings. That restaurant empties its garbage at eight o'clock and ten o'clock. That church gives out free breakfast on Saturdays, and that store sets out its returnable bottles when it closes. Sure beats digging through the garbage cans."

"But how do people stay warm?" Janna asked. She

couldn't imagine not spending a night under her own quilt in her own bed in her very own room.

"Several layers of newspaper inside your coat cut down the wind and will keep you warmer. You can also wad it up to make secondhand shoes fit better. The ubiquitous plastic bag works too, but you make really annoying rustling noises with each step."

"But where do you sleep?"

"Concrete is too cold and hard to spend the night on. Grassy ground is best, but you need to have something waterproof under you to keep the damp out. Damp will chill you faster than outright cold." Eugenie shivered at some memory. Albert patted her shoulder.

They turned up Main Street and stopped outside a soup kitchen. The line of people waiting patiently for a meal was so long that it snaked around the block.

"I thought only grungy old men ate here," Janna said as she eyed the women and children in the line.

"Not anymore," Eugenie said.

Inside the kitchen they watched as an avalanche of powdered mashed potatoes was poured into a garbage can, and Albert had to duck as a woman carrying a canoe paddle came to stir in the water being poured from a five-gallon bucket.

"Gross," Janna said. "I hate instant mashed potatoes."

"Not everybody can order out for pizza whenever they want, Janna," Eugenie said. "Many a night these mashed potatoes kept me fueled up. But since you're so sensitive, we'll move on."

They found themselves on a side street, and Janna looked around anxiously.

"My mom says I shouldn't come down here at night. She says some tough characters hang out here."

Eugenie pointed to a group of about six teenagers singing as they warmed their gloveless hands over a fire in a barrel. They sang with their heads tilted up to the stars, their breath a halo of white smoke above them. They were dressed similarly in lots of black, but their hair was a riot of colors—pink, purple, tufts of orange, and a pale yellow—and various metal piercings glinted in the firelight. *It must really hurt to have a hole made in your lip,* Janna thought. She was a little frightened by their clothes and scruffy looks, but as they sent their voices high into the night sky, the song they sang was catchy and upbeat, and they sang it well. Albert smiled and, moving to the rhythm a little, tried to hit a few of the notes.

"Tough. Oh, my, yes. Quite tough, aren't they?" Then Eugenie pointed to a doorway where an old man sat on the step. He stared straight ahead, unseeing, it seemed, but when the song ended, he clapped his hands slowly.

A man came out of the shop door behind the singers.

"Hey, punks!" he called. "Move it on. You're keeping away the customers."

Grumbling, the kids turned away from the barrel. Cursing at the man, they moved on.

"Why did he do that? They weren't hurting anyone," Albert said. Eugenie didn't answer.

Now that the kids were gone, the old man from the doorstep stood up and tottered down the street.

"Where are we going now?" Janna asked.

"Wherever Judd goes," Eugenie replied, nodding at the old man.

He walked slowly to a delicatessen, opened the door, and stuck his head in. Janna saw the woman behind the counter put her hands on her hips and then make a shooing motion with one hand. Judd closed the door and walked on, bent a little against the chill wind. Judd stood outside of the doorway to a restaurant, approaching people both entering and leaving, holding out his hand. Not one of the people he went up to gave him any money. In fact, they didn't even look at him. After several moments someone from the restaurant came out and motioned him away. Judd's expression didn't change, but the look on Albert's face nearly broke Janna's heart.

Judd pulled his head deeper inside his coat and turned to walk back the other way. Janna saw him take up a place in the soup kitchen line. Then she saw Eugenie watching her.

"Why should I care about a grungy old man? Why doesn't he just get a job?" Janna asked.

"Judd used to have a job—a house and a family, too. First he lost his job, then he lost his house; finally he lost his family. I don't know when he lost his voice. Maybe he just doesn't have much to say anymore. Or he knows nobody will listen."

Janna said nothing.

"Everybody has a story, even grungy old men."

Eugenie motioned for them to sit on a bench by the bus stop.

"I know what you're trying to do to me, Eugenie," Janna said. "It's not going to work. There always have been poor people, and there always will be poor people, and all I know is that I am not going to be one of them."

"Financially poor people, perhaps, but never have I seen such an emotionally destitute existence, whatever the income. Technology can make it so easy to shut out the world." Eugenie seemed to be thinking out loud now. "First people stop talking to other people, then they stop looking at each other. Soon they cease to believe there is any connection between themselves and the rest of humanity."

And indeed, as they sat, watching the passing people, there were no conversations except between people and the cell phones attached to their ears. It seemed as if everyone thought the other bodies were mere obstacles to avoid on their way to where they wanted to go.

"Come on," Eugenie said. She got up and motioned for Janna and Albert to do the same. They walked along in silence until Eugenie stopped at the park entrance.

"Hey, we can't go in there," Janna said. "The park closes at dusk."

"No one can see us. We are here to see, not to be seen, remember?"

They came to a spot sheltered by trees where Janna saw a dark pile in the shadows. As her eyes adjusted, she could see the heads of a woman and a small child wrapped in a blanket. The child had on a hat and a scarf, and Janna could scarcely see his face, but she could hear his small voice.

"Mama?"

"Yes, baby."

"I'm cold."

"I know, pudding. Me too. Think warm thoughts. It will be better tomorrow."

"Why can't we stay at the shelter tonight?"

"We've been there for the last few nights. It's somebody else's turn now."

They heard footsteps in the distance. A policeman approached the two in the dark shadow.

"Oh, no. He'll make them leave," Janna whispered to Eugenie.

"Why are you whispering?" Eugenie asked her. "We

could do a song and dance and they wouldn't notice us." To prove it she waltzed closer and yelled "*Boo*" in the policeman's face. He didn't flinch. Eugenie strode back to Janna.

"We need to stop him," Janna said.

Eugenie shook her head. "No wishes, remember."

"Evening, Ruth," the policeman said.

"Evening, Dale."

"You gonna be okay tonight?" the policeman asked. "Supposed to get pretty nippy."

"We've managed in worse."

"Better have some extra fuel, then." He pulled a couple of sandwiches and candy bars from his jacket pocket and held them out to the woman.

"Thanks, Dale."

"Sleep tight." Dale walked on. "I'll be by later to check on you."

Janna stared. "I thought the cops came through and moved everybody out. I saw it on TV."

"Move them out to where? Sometimes it's safer to be where the cops come through regularly. They turn a blind eye to the ones that won't cause trouble. Maybe they even try to take care of them a little."

"Why doesn't somebody do something?"

"Dale's doing something."

"I mean someone who gets paid to work this kind of thing out—like the mayor or the governor."

"Oh, that's the problem! The head honchos just don't know that some people are having a hard time. Right—I guess they didn't get the memo that people get sick, or lose their jobs, or just fall off the edge a little and somehow can never get back on track. Why don't you go place a few phone calls to let them know what's going on? I'm sure that will fix everything right away."

"Why don't you do something? You're an adult. A very old, experienced, magical adult, quite high up on the career ladder, I might add."

"I would if I could, but stray voltage can't do it. Believe me, I've tried. It doesn't spread. It . . . fizzles out. I can make one large nice thing happen to one person, or maybe two small things, and then boom! I'm fresh out again and freezing my ears."

"Eugenie, I want warm clothes for them. And more food."

"Poof?"

"Yes, poof!" Janna said. "Hurry!"

"Remember our deal. No wishes for twenty-four hours." Eugenie looked at Janna hard.

Janna glared back, then unbuttoned her coat. Her mother would have a fit, but in less than twenty-four hours she would wish herself up a new, prettier one. Quietly she laid the coat on the ground behind Ruth, who had started singing to the little boy.

"Good night," Albert said in a whisper, taking off his

own coat and stuffing a few crumpled bills into the pocket of it before laying it down on top of Janna's.

"We need to go home now," Janna said. "I *hate* being cold."

"Just one more stop," Eugenie said.

Chapter 15

Coatless and shivering, heads hunched between their shoulders against the cold air, Janna and Albert hurried after Eugenie.

"Why can't I just be rich the way I want to be? You're my genie! It's my right!"

"Your right?" Eugenie whirled on Janna. "And what rights does that little boy in the park have? It's hard to remember you're in the land of plenty when I see stuff like that. I may be your genie, and I may not have many rights, but I do have a right to my opinions."

"I'm quite certain this is not appropriate behavior for a genie."

Eugenie sniffed. "So sue me. I understand that's a popular pastime these days, sort of Robin Hood gone wrong with a legal twist to it. Before you blow your genie watts on any more nonsense, I just want you to understand that there are lots of people out there with big, big holes in their hearts, and there are some very rich people living in dire poverty."

They paused in front of a low gray building with peeling paint.

Looking up, Janna was surprised. "Hey, this is our school!"

Eugenie said nothing but held the door open to the school gym and motioned for them to go inside. Janna hurried in and saw the members of the school board seated at a table in front of an audience. In the audience she saw parents of her friends, some neighbors, and a lot of people she didn't know. Janna could see her mother seated with the school board, looking even unhappier than she had looked at home.

"What are we doing here?" Janna asked.

Eugenie just gestured to Janna and Albert to sit down. Mr. Downey, the school principal, whom Janna had only ever heard referred to as "*that wimp*" by her mother, moved to the microphone in front of the school board's table.

"That concludes the presentation of the school board's proposal. As you all know, tomorrow we will vote, yet again, on whether this town will support this budget. We have gone over every line item in detail and have made every effort to cut anything that wasn't absolutely necessary. I would now like to open the floor for discussion."

Immediately the hand of the man sitting in front of

Janna shot into the air. He was a distinguished man with graying hair, and unlike most of the audience, he was dressed in a suit and tie that even Janna recognized as expensive. Janna noticed that the men in the rest of the row looked very similar to this man both in their dress and in their air of solid confidence.

"The board recognizes Mr. Pizer, " Mr. Downey said, although he looked as if he would rather not. Mr. Pizer stood and cleared his throat authoritatively. The other suited men turned their attention to him, respect dripping from their expressions. Mr. Pizer placed a friendly smile on his face and began speaking.

"I would like to applaud the ladies of the board for their efforts. I can only imagine how difficult it must be for nonprofessionals to wrestle with such complicated financial matters." Pizer paused to give them an even wider smile. "However, I'm afraid I must, as a good businessman, point out that many of these budget items simply do not make good business sense."

Mr. Downey's lips thinned. Carol Danner closed her eyes and gripped the edge of the table. Mr. Pizer continued.

"First, such items as the lack of fresh paint on the walls, the flaking plaster from the ceilings, and the chipped floor linoleum are merely cosmetic. These things have not been shown to affect the quality of learning; good minds do not care about the aesthetics of their surroundings.

"Second, the sharing of textbooks and other school equipment that we have heard such commotion about are mere inconveniences. Did inconvenience stop Abe Lincoln? Did it stop any of our forefathers? Of course not! We in the real world know that inconvenience is often merely an incentive for innovation."

There were appreciative murmurs from the suits.

"As far as the request for additional teachers, I feel it my duty to point out that there are no known studies that indicate a smaller class size guarantees a better education. And quite frankly, I find the existing teachers' salaries out of line, and they'd be out of line even if the teachers didn't get the summer off. Why, the fathers of half the kids in this school don't make what the highest-paid teacher makes!"

Mr. Pizer's smile shrunk and his voice grew stern.

"We as a country have grown weak and lazy. It is time for everyone who requests public funds to be accountable to each and every one of us. It is time for schools in particular to tighten their belts before they ask that others do the same. As a concerned citizen, I simply cannot support this request for additional school funds."

The suits broke into applause.

Janna's mother stood up and stepped to the microphone in front of Mr. Downey. Mr. Downey winced.

"Thank you for your views, Mr. Pizer, but I must disagree. When you send thirty-five young people into a classroom where they must wear their coats because of a faulty heating and ventilation system, when students need to have gym class in the hallway because the gym is partitioned into classrooms where the ceiling plaster falls on them as they take an exam, it goes beyond mere 'inconvenience.' It sends a clear message that those in charge don't value the lessons the children are being asked to learn. If we don't value their education more than that, how can we expect them to? How prepared are they going to be to run the world?"

One of the suits leaned to his neighbor. "Run the world? Run a cash register, maybe!"

"You want fries with that shake?" his neighbor replied, and they erupted in laughter.

Carol's voice took on an edge. "We know that as a successful businessman, Mr. Pizer, you understand investments and 'complicated financial matters,' as you call them. I would like to point out that children are not pieces of real estate. Nor are they a get-rich-quick scheme. This school's belt is quite tight, Mr. Pizer. Tighter than yours, I guarantee. You make ten times what the highest-paid teacher in this school does."

"Everything I have I've worked for." Pizer's voice rose and had a nasty note in it. "I am a self-made man, Ms. Danner."

"No one is self-made, Mr. Pizer. We all had someone somewhere who invested in us. Teachers, coaches, neighbors, friends. It's payback time. Good teachers are prepared to enlighten and inspire, but we must give them adequate tools. As a country we seem to value the plumber more than the ones who care for our babies and small children, and we pay our auto mechanics more than those who shape our nation's ability to create and compete. Certainly, as a good businessman, creativity and competition are important to you."

"With all due respect," Pizer said, "I don't believe that Ms. Danner is qualified to grasp the business principles at work here—"

"With all due respect," Carol interrupted, "I don't believe that you are qualified to grasp that this is not about business principles."

Mr. Downey looked slightly ill. The men seated with Pizer shuffled their feet and shifted in their seats.

"We're talking about the future of a planet," she went on. Her voice shook a little, and Janna realized with surprise that her mother was nervous, maybe even frightened. "If we don't believe our children are worth this investment, how are they ever going to believe it?"

"I value education very highly, Ms. Danner."

"The private school your daughter went to wasn't troubled by such inconveniences as requesting public funds, was it? What about all the other children, Mr. Pizer?"

Carol Danner turned to the audience. "I don't know about you folks, but I'm worn out at the end of the day.

Mr. Pizer may have the benefit of a physical trainer's services followed by a private massage, but I bet none of you sitting out there does. We have to manage without such perks, and then come out on nights like this too because we need to watch out for our children's future."

Janna saw people in the audience exchange glances, and heard a few murmurs. A man in a bow tie stood up and raised his hand hesitantly. With a start Janna recognized Albertoo.

"Excuse me. Albert DellaRosa. Permission to speak?" He nodded to Mr. Downey, who nodded back, looking relieved at the diversion. "I've run a few numbers, and it's the most fascinating thing!" Janna heard Albert groan next to her. Albertoo's fascinating things had a way of making people nod off.

"The budget increase is about the cost of renting a movie each week. Isn't the education of a generation worth that to us?" He looked around at the crowd, nodding encouragingly. Some just stared back; some nodded a little uncertainly.

"Who do you think needs that movie more at the end of the week, Mr. Pizer?" Albertoo's voice took on some strength. "You, or those of us who work full-time to provide for our families, and with the time left we volunteer, instead of have a private training session, because we know that you can't raise a generation on business principles?"

"It's simply a matter of priorities—"

"Mr. Pizer, we know where our priorities are. And now I think we all know where yours are. I see too many young people not finishing school, unable to get decent work so that they, in turn, can reach down and pull up the next batch. For our society to heal itself and thrive, we must invest in all children, not just our own. How well the world is managed tomorrow depends on the self-respect and confidence we build in these children today. This budget is not about paint, or textbooks, or really even teachers' salaries. It's about a better future. I may be an accountant, but I know that the things that really count aren't things you can count."

Pizer clenched his jowls before responding.

"Times are hard, Mr. DellaRosa."

Albertoo stared at him for a few seconds, and in that few seconds Janna felt she had never really looked at him before. The goofy expression he usually had on his face had vanished. His chin was set and his eyes were hard.

"For whom, Mr. Pizer?" Albertoo said, and then sat down.

Albert stared at his dad for a moment. He nudged Janna. "Isn't he just the coolest man alive?"

A hand shot up from the audience, and Mr. Downey gratefully acknowledged it. "Ms. Hibbs, you have a comment?"

"I move that this meeting be adjourned. I think we've all heard quite enough."

"Second!" came an eager voice.

Mr. Downey looked helplessly around. Janna's mother sat down and began collecting her papers, pushing her hair from her face.

"Meeting adjourned," Mr. Downey squeaked, but nobody was listening.

Mr. Pizer made his way rather huffily toward the gym door. His friends stood up as a group and scuttled after him. Janna, Eugenie, and Albert followed them. They watched as Pizer and one of the men accompanying him walked toward a Mercedes with the license plate DESERVD on it.

"How did she know about my daughter? And how could she possibly have guessed that I'd just had a massage?"

"Well, those things do get around the office," replied his companion with a little embarrassment.

Pizer stared at him with incomprehension.

"She does work for you, you know," his minion said.

"That woman works at Pizer Industries?" Pizer asked, his voice high with disbelief.

"She's an analyst. She's quite good, I hear."

"Fire her."

There was a silence. "Excuse me, sir?"

"You heard what I said."

"Sir, we've already ensured that the budget won't pass. We bought enough votes to guarantee it. Isn't firing her a little over the—"

Pizer interrupted. "Just see that she never gets a pay-check from me again."

The men climbed into the car.

"Fire her?" Janna shrieked as she strode toward the Mercedes, but the engine roared and her voice was lost. "You can't fire my mom! Don't you dare! What's the matter? Can't stand a little opposition? Come out here where I can talk to you! I'll give you opposition!"

Eugenie and Albert each grabbed one of Janna's arms and pulled her away from the car. It sped off.

"Stop the car! Eugenie, make him take it back! I wish for you to have him not fire my mother! I wish . . . I wish for him to give her a raise! I wish for him to . . . make her president of the company!"

"No wishes for twenty-four hours," Eugenie said firmly. "Besides, she'd be much better off not working for the likes of him. Now that he knows who she is, he'll make her working days miserable. I know his type."

"I need to go home," Janna said, shivering. Her mind was filled with everything she had seen, and all she wanted was to be in her own bedroom. Albert shivered in agreement and slung an awkward arm around her to warm them both up.

"Pity you gave up your coats. We could have had a lot more fun," Eugenie said.

"Fun? We see poor people freezing to death, you show us people trying to cheat us out of an education, my mom gets fired, and you call that fun?" Janna asked.

"You saw poverty surrounded by plenty, yes, but you also saw some uplifting things: generosity in response to hardship, courage in the face of a selfish power."

"If that's the uplifting stuff, I can't imagine despair," Albert said.

"When you have seen the real world, you either harden your heart like Pizer and let each day layer another thickness onto your shell or you face that you are a part of this life and you embrace the full catastrophe, the glop, the mess, the pain, and the sweetness, and you do what you can. Besides, your mom isn't fired yet. Anything can happen."

"I admit that there are a lot of people in worse shape than I am," Janna said slowly, "but . . . " She trailed off.

They walked back to Janna's house. For once Eugenie was quiet.

At the door Janna turned to Eugenie.

"What is it that you want me to do? Not, of course, that I will. I'm just curious."

"Well, I don't know, exactly." Eugenie had the grace to look embarrassed.

Janna stared at her. "You mean to tell me that all this

time you've been harassing me about making a difference, you haven't had a clue how to do it?"

"You're the first one I've had any success with. Being a genie is a little like living in a democracy—I don't have much power on my own so I have to work indirectly through my designated representative. But since I don't even get to *vote*, I've never had to work out the details. Besides, the genie oath prohibits me from offering wish-specific guidance. I could have my bag yanked, with me in it."

"Oh, great! You can pressure me, guilt-trip me, and badger me, but you can't offer me advice?" Janna was so angry she forgot to shiver.

"Isn't there a reference manual?" Albert asked. "Or a tech support hotline?"

"I'll settle for a *Genies for Dummies* book," Janna said. When Eugenie shook her head, a little miserably, Janna asked, "Have any of your masters ever, ever tried to make a difference?"

"Well, none of *mine*, but I do know that a few, a very few, did somehow manage to turn their good fortune into something with a life of its own. It grew and grew, well beyond the thousand-genie-watt capacity—sort of like endless good vibrations. You're a little too young for that song, though, aren't you?" Eugenie started snapping her fingers and doing a little move with her hips, humming. "How did that go now?"

Albert nodded in recognition, closing his eyes to look for the right rhythm.

"Stop it! Both of you!" Janna snapped. "When was the last time that happened?"

"The sixties. You don't think that flower power did it all on its lonesome, do you?"

"What was the wish? Who wished it?"

"All wish data is strictly confidential. You have to have a higher security clearance than I have to get at it." Eugenie sighed.

"But what if I want to make that kind of wish?"

"I don't know any more than you do, but I think it needs to come from renewable energy—'sustainable' is the buzzword nowadays—and it needs to have some way of hopping around the world. I don't think it's a complete coincidence that the way mortals tap into genie power is by being kind, but that's as far as I've gotten." On seeing Janna's fallen face, Eugenie rushed on like a car salesman. "It just needs a little work. I know you can do it, Janna."

"Maybe one global superwish?" Albert said. "Like . . . nobody makes mistakes?"

Eugenie whacked him with her cane. "How would you learn anything, then?"

"How about a cure for cancer?" Janna suggested.

"Or make all cars run on alternative fuel, right now, this minute?" Albert said.

"Those are all single problems. I think you need to

think multivector," Eugenie said. "Think big, think wide, think connected, think web. I don't believe specific problems are the problem, it's the way they're handled."

"That's the kind of thing my mother says when I'm having trouble with homework."

"So, think of it as homework." Eugenie patted Janna on the shoulder and turned to go. "I got a message from Steve and need to check in. I expect it's about my overdue fifty-thousand-mile checkup. I'll be back tomorrow afternoon."

Chapter 16

Janna went to her room and surveyed the results of her wishes. Why did the things look larger and more colorful in the catalog than they did in her room? And why did the kids in the photographs look happier to have them than she felt?

She tried to get involved in *The Secret Princess*, but somehow it lost its appeal when she thought about Ruth and her son. She wondered where Judd would spend the night, and if the teenagers were still out there somewhere, sending musical messages up to the cold night stars. Then she thought about how tired her mother had looked at the school board meeting.

When she heard her mother arrive home and Janna's ill-gotten gains had obediently become invisible again, she closed the door to her bedroom and went downstairs. Her mother hung up her coat and turned on the teakettle in silence. She sat down at the table to wait for the water to heat and slowly put her face into her hands. Janna realized that her mother wasn't even aware that she was in the room.

"Hi, Mom," Janna said quietly.

Her mother instantly straightened up and put on a smile. "I didn't hear you come in. How was your evening?"

Janna thought of all the possible replies to that question. *Albert and I appeared invisibly in the Newbys' living room, I gave a little boy the coat you just bought me, and I know you're getting fired tomorrow.* She settled on, "Fine. How was yours?"

"Discouraging."

"Is the budget going to pass tomorrow?"

"No."

"Why won't Pizer help fix our school?"

Janna's mother thought a moment, and then said slowly, "I honestly don't know. I think that only unhappy people try to hurt other people, and that's why it's so hard to be stingy if you're basically a happy person. Happy people just aren't capable of being mean."

"How could someone like Pizer be unhappy? He can have anything he wants."

Carol threw up her hands. "I don't know, Janna. He could give so much to so many people. Instead he hoards it, and the thought of losing a few bucks makes him miserable enough to be nasty."

The kettle began to sing, and Carol got up.

Janna nodded her head in silence, and then said, "Good night, Mom."

"Night, baby."

At the bottom of the stairs Janna stopped and turned around.

"Mom?"

"Yes?"

"How would you make the world a better place?"

Janna expected her mother to think a while on the question, but she just smiled and said, "It's a pretty wonderful place just the way it is."

"How can you say that, given the way we live?"

Carol stared at her daughter. "What's wrong with the way we live?"

"Beat-up car, used clothes . . . " Janna trailed off at the look on her mother's face.

"I'm sorry you think the way we live is so awful, Janna." There was a hint of a smile on her face, but it was a sad kind of smile.

"I didn't mean it like that."

Janna's mother looked at her but didn't say anything. Janna tried again.

"How come some people have way more than they need when others have to go to bed cold and hungry?"

Carol eyed her daughter. "You're asking some very

difficult questions tonight. Is there anything . . . in particular going on?"

Janna had the sudden urge to tell her mother everything, right down to the genie's black galoshes. Instead, she just shook her head.

Her mother paused a moment, then said, "If everybody understood that we are all connected, and that everybody has the power to change the world, I'm quite certain that the rest would take care of itself."

"But wouldn't everybody want to change the world so it's a better place just for them and no one else?" Janna asked.

Janna's mother shook her head. "If you really believe that you are connected to everyone else, then you understand that when you give what you can, you also get what you need. What goes around comes around."

"But, what could *I* give anybody?" Janna's mind was spinning in frustration, and the question came out almost as a wail. She had a lot of things upstairs, but she couldn't imagine what Ruth would do with a life-size cardboard cutout of Pit Bullard.

"The best gifts are not in boxes, Janna. Some people have time, some people have money, but how you behave to someone can be a gift too, and it's within everyone's power to just be decent. Everyone makes a difference."

"How can you know that?"

Her mother shrugged. "The way you know anything really important—you just know."

Janna nodded and then went upstairs, leaving her mother to sip her tea in silence, staring thoughtfully into the darkness that her daughter had vanished into.

Before she went to sleep that night, Janna thought about a lot of things. About Elizabeth's finery. About Mr. Pizer's money and his flashy car with the obnoxious vanity plate. What was it that people like him wished for in the still of the night? She didn't have a clue.

She heard the wind gain momentum outside her window and wondered what it felt like to go to bed cold and hungry. When she finally fell asleep, she dreamed strange dreams. Mr. Pizer sat on one end of a teeter-totter, his feet firmly on the ground. He somehow managed to keep the entire school board up in the air on the other end of the teeter-totter, their legs angrily kicking and flailing. Then a huge Möbius strip appeared and all sorts of people climbed aboard. Mr. Pizer chased Mr. Downey, and Mr. Downey chased Elizabeth, and Elizabeth chased Judd, and Judd chased Ruth and her son, and Ruth and her son chased the six teenage singers, and they chased Mr. Pizer, like a huge and comical game at recess, until they all fell down laughing.

Janna woke up and stared out her window at the night sky. She used to think it great fun to watch the stars appear as the sky darkened. Her mother had taught her to chant:

Star light, star bright,
First star I see tonight,
I wish I may, I wish I might,
Have this wish I wish tonight.

She had never had a shortage of wishes before, but she had never really believed the wishes would come true. Now that she knew she could make one wish that could change the world, that particular wish eluded her.

Chapter 17

Janna's night was short, and her sleep was restless, but when her alarm went off in the morning, she sat upright in bed, wide awake. She had the answer, it *had* to be the answer. If it wasn't, it would use up all her genie watts anyway, and this time Eugenie couldn't give them back. It was their only chance.

She dressed and ate breakfast quickly, aware that her mother was shooting her concerned looks.

"I'm all right, really," she said, in response to Carol's wordless questioning hand on her daughter's forehead.

"I've left you some dinner in the refrigerator. I was going to stay at the polling booths until the votes were all counted tonight, but I'll come home sooner if you're not feeling well."

"I'm fine, Mom."

With a last worried glance at her daughter, Carol left for work.

Janna had to dig out last year's coat to wear to school but didn't even notice the frayed cuffs and ripped pocket.

She couldn't concentrate in math class, she toyed with her lunch, and got hit in the head with a basketball in gym because she was staring into space. After school she ran home, bursting in the front door.

"Eugenie! Eugenie!"

She ran upstairs and found Eugenie lying down on her bed reading a tabloid that screamed PIT BULLARD HOSPITALIZED WITH HALLUCINATIONS!

"I've got it!"

"It had better be good," Eugenie said morosely. "Somebody snitched and I got a huge lecture from Genie Central. They might suspend me."

"Why did I have to get the only activist genie in existence?" Janna asked.

"Just lucky, I guess," Eugenie said, sitting up.

Janna reached over and patted Eugenie's hand. They smiled at each other.

Eugenie seemed to pull herself together, and a vestige of the old vim appeared.

"They'll see. All revolutions start small, after all. So, what is it that you've 'got'?"

"Follow my logic for a minute," Janna said excitedly. "If there really is enough in the world to go around, but the balance is all wrong, we just need to shift it a little. Just like weight on a teeter-totter."

Eugenie squinted tiredly. "Nobody has ever quite solved the distribution of wealth problem satisfactorily. Nobody. Ever."

"But it's not just wealth that needs to be redistributed. It's time, and kindness, and love and attention. Everybody has something to give."

"Sounds a little trite," Eugenie said.

Janna waved her hand impatiently. "Remember when I had you wish for what you wanted?"

Eugenie nodded.

"Can I give other people wishes too?" Janna asked. "Can I wish them genie watts for a wish of their own? A sort of wishing wish?"

"I suppose. I've never been asked to do that before."

"Don't you see?" Janna said. "If I give wishing wishes to a bunch of different people, then they in turn will want to reach out and give to someone else, and they'll pass on the goodwill like the common cold. Maybe they'll even wish for something on someone else's behalf! We'll start a chain reaction that eventually, because we are all connected in some way, will reach everybody everywhere. It will be like your grumpy epidemic, only in reverse."

"I don't know. It sounds too simple and too complicated all at the same time."

"You were the one preaching connectivity and balance when all I wanted was a houseful of Neiman Marcus."

Eugenie paused. "What if it doesn't work?"

Janna shrugged. "Then I tried. I don't have any other ideas." She tilted her head at Eugenie. "Any idea how far a thousand genie watts will go?"

"I don't have a clue. You'll have to go slowly or I might overheat."

"You mean, like, blow up?"

"Maybe."

"Cool."

Eugenie gave Janna a hurt look.

"How long do you think it will take to find out if it works?"

"Again, I don't have a clue."

"You're not a very good genie, are you?"

"Oh, no, I'm a very good genie. I'm just a rather poor fortune-teller."

"So, let's do it," Janna said. "First we need to get Albert."

"Why?"

"If Albert misses this, he will never forgive me—no matter how it turns out."

"What happened to '*It's just Albert. Who cares what he thinks*'?" Eugenie mimicked Janna's whine too closely for comfort.

"I've always needed Albert, ever since his diaper exploded."

Eugenie smiled.

"Eugenie, I wish Albert here."

Albert appeared sprawled on the floor.

He looked from Eugenie to Janna. "Don't ever do that again."

"Not to worry," Janna said. "I'm going to burn through all thousand genie watts tonight. Eugenie thinks she might blow up. I figured you'd want to watch."

"Can I go back and get my video camera?" Albert asked.

Eugenie gave him a nasty look. She cleared her throat and waved at the spoils of Janna's catalog sprees.

"In order to give you your thousand watts back, I need to repossess all this stuff."

Albert looked in amazement at Janna's wish booty. He picked up the tricycle and looked at Janna, a question mark on his face.

"I never had a red one," she said, as if that explained everything.

Janna sighed and gave it all one last glance. She stroked the large teddy bear and ran her hand across the gorgeous teal sweater that brought out the blue in her eyes.

"I wish for all of this to go back where it came from."

Eugenie looked at her. "Are you certain?"

"Poof," Janna said, nodding.

And *poof*, it was all gone. She was going to have to wait a long time to find out how *The Secret Princess* ended.

"I wish," Janna started—then she stopped. "Wait, if I'm going to do this properly, I need a wand. Eugenie, I wish for a wand."

"Poof," Eugenie said, and a glowing wand appeared in Janna's hand.

"I wish that Albert gets the first wishing wish," Janna said. "Go on, whatever you want."

Albert looked blank. "Can I think about it awhile? I don't want to screw it up."

"Do you think the wishing wish will really reach everyone?" Janna asked.

Eugenie shrugged. "It may miss a few people who aren't really connected to anyone, like some lawyers and most politicians, but, hey—"

"I thought I'd start with people close by, so we can see what happens. Let's go outside and get started," Janna said.

They walked out of Janna's house, where she closed her eyes and said solemnly, "I wish for Mrs. Newby and Elizabeth to get whatever they want most right now." Janna turned to Eugenie. "There. We ought to see a Laura Ashley truck drive up any minute."

"Hold on to your patootie!" Eugenie whispered. And then more loudly she said, "Poof! Poof!"

Janna opened her eyes cautiously, and they eyed one another in silence.

"How—How will we know if it worked?" Janna asked.

"The results may not be immediately visible. We may just have to trust it for a bit. Go ahead. Wish for somebody else."

Janna watched seven-year-old Erica from up the block struggle to balance on the new mountain bike she'd gotten for Christmas. She had seen Erica out several times before, trying to get the hang of it, and inevitably crashing. Fortunately, snow banks are soft.

Quietly, Janna intoned, "I wish that Erica gets what she is wishing for right now."

Before their eyes Erica's bike ceased to wobble. She sat up in the seat, straight and sure, and pedaled mightily past them.

"Look at me!" Erica shrieked as she cruised by. "Look at me!"

Janna, Albert, and Eugenie looked at one another.

"I'm not sure that was the learning experience for her that it should have been," Albert said.

"Shut up, Albert," Janna and Eugenie said.

They watched Erica as she barreled up her driveway and confidently made the turn. She hopped off her bike and joyously hugged the tiny dog lying in the snow, then ran into the house to tell her mother the good news. She reappeared almost immediately and gave the dog a bone that was nearly as big as it was. After dispensing another quick hug to the pooch, Erica ran back into the house. Janna laughed out loud.

"Well, that was certainly immediate," Eugenie said.

Just then Mr. Newby's car turned down the street. He waved gaily to Janna, Albert, and Eugenie.

Janna stared. “Mr. Newby never waves. I thought he needed glasses for the first three months they lived there because he never seemed to see me.”

Eugenie grabbed Janna’s arm. “Look!”

Mr. Newby hopped out of the car bearing a large armful of flowers. He trotted up his walkway and was met at the door by an amazed Mrs. Newby.

Janna and Eugenie exchanged glances.

“Do you think . . . ?” Janna began.

“Nah, couldn’t be. . . . He must be just feeling really, really guilty about something.”

“Let’s take a walk,” Janna said, and headed down the sidewalk. She pointed to a faded yellow house as they passed it.

“Let’s see what’s going on there,” Janna said. They crept to the living room picture window.

Inside, Mrs. Watson stood in a glazed stupor as she surveyed her shambles of a house. With three young children and four pets, there was no catching up. There were toys all over the living room floor, four baskets of dirty laundry, two sinks full of dirty dishes. The baby on her hip shrieked mercilessly. Mrs. Watson closed her eyes for a moment to regain her strength.

“I wish for Mrs. Watson to get what she is wishing for most right now,” Janna said, and waved her wand.

When Mrs. Watson opened her eyes, the house was miraculously clean. Even the magazines were straightened and the garbage had been taken out. The baby swallowed its next bellow in sheer surprise.

"I don't know his name, but a little boy just moved into that new pseudo-Tudor. Let's give him a wish."

They walked to the house and lurked outside a picture window, watching as the father put down his newspaper and addressed his son.

"You know, buddy, I've decided I'm not going away this weekend after all," they heard him say. "Let's do something you want to do."

"This is all very well and good," Janna said as they walked away, "but I'm not sure some father-son time here and a clean house there are going to change the world."

"Patience, dear," was all Eugenie said.

They passed the Third Citizen's Bank. "Poof," Janna said, waving her wand at it.

"What was that for?" Albert asked.

"Just a random act of kindness," Janna said.

"But . . . how do we know who got what?" Albert said.

Janna eyed him. "What part of 'random' don't you understand?"

"What if there was nobody in there who wanted something?" he said.

"Everybody wants something, and besides, it won't use any watts if nobody uses the wish."

Albert turned to Eugenie. "Don't you need to see the same people for her to pass on watts?"

"It helps, but it isn't necessary," Eugenie said.

"But what if two people in there want diametrically opposed things?" Albert said. "What happens then?"

Eugenie shrugged. "We're in unknown territory, but I'd guess that if they both can't have what they want, it just comes down to who wants their wish more."

"I still think you're being wasteful," Albert said to Janna. He pointed down the street. "Maybe we can do some *visible* good at the hospital."

When they entered the hospital lobby, the woman at the desk was arguing on the phone. "You never do what you say you're going to do, and I'm always the one who gets up early—"

Janna leaned toward Eugenie, whispered to her, and twitched her wand. The woman broke off suddenly. "I love you, too," she said, apropos of nothing.

"Let's go to the emergency room," Albert said.

"Are we allowed to?" Janna asked.

"We'll just say our great-grandmother here is feeling faint."

Eugenie sneered but went with them as they followed the signs to the ER. Janna remembered her last visit there clearly, having been down at the river barefoot the previous summer in spite of promising her mother never to go shoeless there. Needless to say, a piece of broken glass had found her soft foot and she had needed seven stitches. That had been bad enough, but the worst thing had been the sound of a small child screaming as the doctor had tried to remove something stuck inside his ear canal. All it took was the smell of the hospital to make Janna queasy now.

Albert elbowed Janna and pointed to the motley collection of people in the waiting room. A teenage girl wearing a leotard under her coat had obviously been crying and held her arm very carefully. A worried young man held a little boy who whimpered occasionally, his eyes closed. An older man with a gray, strained face sat in a wheelchair, wheezing and occasionally coughing deeply. His wife held his hand tightly and looked scared. The middle-aged man slumped in a chair holding his head in his hands was the first to react. He lifted his head carefully and blinked, then straightened and inhaled deeply, a confused yet relieved expression on his face. He stood up, shook himself, and walked out. Then the teenage girl began carefully moving her arm, a look of wonder on her face. She gulped and touched delicately where the pain had been, then smiled.

Albert grinned and gave Janna a thumbs-up. The old man gave a tremendous bark, making them all jump, but after that his breathing was calm and a better color started coming back to his face. The little boy sat up in his father's lap and giggled at something. They were about to leave when they heard the sound of an ambulance approaching. There was a clatter as it pulled up to the ER doors and the attendants called out in their staccato serious jargon. Janna hoped it wasn't bloody. She hated blood. The desk nurse came running up, and the paramedics looked intense and focused as they silently and quickly began to unload their patient. She didn't see any blood, but Janna knew that so much intensity and focus wasn't a good sign. The inert figure on the stretcher suddenly began to pull at the mask on his face.

"I'm all right," he said. The paramedics stopped; the desk nurse stopped.

"No, you're not," one of the paramedics said. "You've suffered a massive coronary."

"You must be mistaken," the man said, sitting up and noting his surroundings with some curiosity. "I've never felt better in my life."

In the confusion, Janna, Albert, and Eugenie slipped outside into the night.

"Not a bad day's work," Eugenie said.

"But it isn't working fast enough," Janna said. "There's no way this is going to spread far enough!"

"Let's see what else we can find to do," Albert said. They left the hospital and headed downtown. They saw the same group of teenagers from the night before huddled over the barrel fire, clapping their hands but apparently too cold to sing. They saw Judd sitting on the same doorstep. Clearly nothing had changed here.

Janna pointed to the kids.

"I wish them to be warm."

The same man from yesterday opened the door of the shop behind them.

"Hey, you kids!" he hollered.

The kids stopped their clapping but didn't move. There was a tension in the air Janna didn't like.

"Hurry!" Albert said to Eugenie. Eugenie shrugged her shoulders, palms up.

"I already poofed," she whispered.

"Well, poof harder, then!" Albert said.

"It's chilly out here," the shopkeeper said. He paused, a little uncertain of what he was doing, but he knew why. "You'd better come in for some hot chocolate."

The kids looked at him in amazement, and then, exchanging uncertain glances, they entered the shop.

Albert pointed to Judd on the doorstep. Janna nodded at him.

"I wish for Judd to have something good to eat."

"Poof."

A moment later they watched as the lady from the delicatessen came out to the street. She gave Judd a large brown bag.

"Come see me tomorrow," she said. "It's calzone day and I'll save a couple for you."

Judd opened the bag and delved in hungrily. A scrawny mutt slunk up beside him, and Judd gave the dog a roll.

"Did you see that?" Albert said. "He passed it on. It's working!"

"Giving a pooch a treat isn't going to keep my mother from losing her job. Oh, this is a stupid idea!"

Eugenie nudged Janna, and Janna turned to see her coat coming up the street on Ruth, the woman from the park. Her son trundled beside her, looking hilarious in Albert's overlarge coat. Judd saw them too. He closed the brown bag and ambled up to the two.

"Please, I've had all I can eat," he said, holding out the bag. "Take this for you and your son."

Albert cocked his head at Janna. "I think it's starting to take off."

"Albert's right," Eugenie said. "I've felt a couple shocks, like my system is overloading."

"Maybe if you spend the watts as fast as you can, the momentum will increase," Albert suggested to Janna.

"Hey!" Eugenie complained. "I say I'm overloading and you say go faster?"

Janna had a sudden thought. "Come on," she said. "We need to go to your house, Albert."

"Why my house?"

"Because unlike poor, pitiful me, *you* have cable!"

Chapter 18

They settled themselves on the DellaRosa futon. Albert turned the TV on with a remote control and surfed until he found a news channel. Two talking heads, Clive and Marilee, were looking somber as they gave a rundown of the day's headlines. Janna generally avoided the news as much as possible, as it seemed to her that the same bad things happened each day in the world, just someplace different, and . . . how did it really affect her after all? But now she sat and she listened and she watched.

"In spite of ongoing efforts to reach a peace agreement, the summit has devolved into riots after a car bomb exploded outside the main mosque. . . ." Marilee's voice narrated film footage of fire and wreckage and frightened people running. Janna raised her wand and wished.

Albert shook his head.

Janna turned to look at him. "You don't believe this will work, do you?"

Albert shook his head again.

"Well, *I* do," Janna said. And she turned back to concentrate on the news.

"Over to you, Clive," Marilee said.

Albert leaned over to Eugenie. "That's the look Janna got right before she slugged Gail Goldstein in kindergarten when she wanted Gail's yellow place mat. I don't want to be around when she finds out her princess wand doesn't have the mojo she thinks it should have."

Eugenie looked at him, a little wide-eyed, then turned back to watch with Janna.

"In the local news," Clive said, "the temperature coupled with precipitation is spelling tragedy on the highway, where an eight-car collision just took place. Emergency workers are rushing to the scene as we speak. We'll have film and commentary at our nightly update."

There was a brief look at a fuzzy interstate scene.

"Brrr," Clive said, and chuckled to Marilee. "Bet they all wish they'd gone to Florida."

Marilee furrowed her brow at him, and his grin faltered, but only for a second. Music swelled, the cameras backed off, and Marilee and Clive smiled in unison. "Until ten, make it a great day."

Albert cycled through the channels. A local car dealer shouted his own praises. There were ads for various health remedies and other television shows, a few public service announcements, and a number of laugh tracks that sounded oddly the same. Janna sighed and waved her wand vaguely. Eugenie started to look a little glassy-eyed.

"What next?" Albert asked. "Or have you worn your wrist out waving that wand?"

Janna sunk her chin into her hands. "I . . . I don't know what else to do. It sounded so . . . possible, but now . . . "

Eugenie patted Janna's knee. "Rome wasn't built in a day, dear."

"I've always thought that was a particularly unhelpful sentiment," Janna said.

Eugenie nodded. "Perhaps it is. The point is that you tried. You did what you could."

"What do you mean I *did* what I could? Can't I do anything more?"

"I don't know what it would be, dear," Eugenie said. "Goodness, I am tired." She pulled her knees up onto the futon, leaned against Janna's shoulder, and promptly fell asleep.

Janna looked as though she were going to cry, but Albert just shrugged and scanned the channels until he found a superhero marathon. Janna watched it mutely, wondering how she'd come to be in this odd situation, if it would scar her permanently, and how best to help her mother deal with being unemployed. And then she, too, drifted off. Wishing was hard work.

She woke up to snorty noises from a dream of trying to ride a magic rug. The snorting rug turned out to be Eugenie, who was waking up from her own apparently disturbing dream. They righted themselves and stretched as Albert began cycling through the channels again. It was time for the ten o'clock news.

"In a nearly statistically impossible luck of the draw," Marilee said, "*all* of the jackpots were won tonight, and the Lottery Commission says that they will be closing down temporarily to test their equipment. Over to you, Clive."

"And in another freak occurrence, all local high school basketball games ended in ties."

All three of them stared at the television. Albert clicked to another station.

" . . . and a major pharmaceutical company has announced plans to go nonprofit."

Click. A map appeared.

"Meanwhile, on the global front, this country's regime, long suspected of dictatorial crimes against humanity, decided to step down so its members can spend more time with their families."

Click.

"Stayed tuned for surprising late-breaking news. And now this from our sponsor!"

"Do you think . . . ?" Janna ventured. They suffered through an ad—none of them could figure out for what—and then a solemn-faced, soberly dressed, and highly paid newsman said in a deep and serious voice:

"Peace erupted in the latest Mideastern conflict. The details are unclear, but we do have a quote from the commanding officer of Alpha Strike Force."

The camera shot to a battle-toughened military man. "We suddenly realized that all of us just wanted to stop fighting and get on with our lives," he said, a look of wonderment on his face. "So we did. Yeah."

Click.

Clive's face filled the screen again. "A lot of strange stories out there today, but this one has my vote for the weirdest," he said. A grainy black-and-white video of the inside of the Third Citizen's Bank appeared on the TV screen.

Albert nudged Janna and Eugenie. "There's the bank you poofed! Maybe they found gold in the vault, or . . ."

Inside the bank that was walking distance from where they were now, which had been nearly empty in the late afternoon hour, a masked bank robber held a gun on a frightened teller. Suddenly he put his gun down and stood there, apparently confused.

"Excuse me," he apologized. "I don't know what got into me."

"No problem. Think nothing of it," the teller replied. "Would you like to open a totally free checking account with us today?"

Off camera, Marilee giggled, definitely not a scripted giggle, and Clive looked a little disconcerted.

"Nice job pointing the wand of random kindness," Albert said.

The camera panned to Marilee, who had recovered her poise. "And another happy ending: That eight-car pileup we mentioned earlier resulted in no injuries. Ambulance crews stated they were amazed that each person involved, including this one"—here the camera showed a car accordioned into an impossibly twisted crush of metal from which an elderly man emerged and calmly brushed himself off—"was able to walk away unassisted."

"Looks like some car dealer is going to get lucky tomorrow, though," Clive said, and grinned. Marilee shot him a disapproving glance.

"This is only the stuff we know about. Imagine the stories that didn't make the news," Albert said.

He was right.

"We did it. We really did something," Janna said, sinking back into the futon. She looked at Eugenie. "And you didn't even explode."

"There were a few sparks at one point," Eugenie confessed, "but I patted them out."

Eugenie stood and stretched. "I hate to break up this little piece of history, but I need to get back to my bag. I feel like I've run a marathon. I'm too old for this kind of a blitzkrieg."

Albert turned the TV off, and they looked at one another, smiling, for a few silent seconds. It was hard to believe it was over, but then, it was hard to believe, period.

"I wonder if anything has changed between your house and mine," Albert said. "I'll walk you guys home."

Slowly they made their way back to Janna's house. Inside the neighborhood houses they could see shadows of people dancing, they could hear music, and they saw silhouettes of people's heads leaning together over tables. Instead of turning up the Danners' walk, Eugenie motioned for them to follow her over to the Newbys' house. They crept to the window and peeked in. In front of the fireplace there was a Monopoly board laid out, and around it were Mr. and Mrs. Newby and Elizabeth, who was resting one arm on Barney. The three of them were talking animatedly about who was going to get Boardwalk first.

"Wasn't that sweet?" Albert said as they headed back to Janna's house. "Talk about getting out of jail free, huh?"

"It was nauseating," Janna said.

"You *are* a little overly sentimental, dear boy," Eugenie said, with a small pat to Albert's back.

It was then that it washed over Janna like a wave—how very, very much she possessed—the depth and breadth and wealth and warmth of all that surrounded her. She knew then that she was the one who had gotten out of jail free.

Albert began humming as they walked. It took Janna a few moments to place the melody as the one Ruth had sung to lullaby her son to sleep.

"So that's what a thousand genie watts will accomplish," Eugenie said dreamily.

Janna stopped short. "You mean they're all gone?"

"You ran out a while ago, someplace in China, I think. This thing's going on its own momentum now." Eugenie saw the look on Janna's face. "What's wrong?"

"I wanted to give my mom a wish," Janna said. "Aren't there even just a couple watts left to save her from getting fired?"

"I'm in enough trouble already. I'm sorry." Eugenie sighed. She stared at Janna as a thought occurred to her. "Come to think of it, you didn't make a wish for yourself, either."

Janna shrugged. "I think . . . I think I have everything I really want." She looked at Albert. "What did you end up wishing for, Albert? You *did* manage to make a wish before we ran out, right?"

"Yes, I made a wish," Albert said quietly. He pushed his glasses up and looked away.

"I bet you're going to be the next Jimi Hendrix!" Janna whooped, clapping her hands. "All those pictures I've got of you from your nerd days will make me a fortune."

Albert murmured something.

"What?" Janna asked.

"I said, actually I wished for the school budget to pass."

"*The school budget?*" Janna shook her head. "If you didn't want to be a rock star, why not go for a Nobel Prize? For the DellaRosa Theorem of . . . of Pi or something?"

Albert set his chin and looked away.

"Don't worry, Albert," Eugenie said, "that Nobel Prize will be all the sweeter for winning it on your own."

They saw Janna's mother's car turn up the street. Janna took a deep breath.

"You want me to go with you?" Albert asked.

"No. I guess not. Thanks." They tapped knuckles, and Albert turned to go, but he turned back and looked at her. It was as if Janna had never seen him before. When you've known someone for so long, you forget how they look, because they look so . . . *like themselves* that you never stop to think if they are handsome or cool or young-looking, until some little thing tilts your vision slightly and, suddenly, there they are just as everyone else sees them. In that sudden second Janna saw a hint of the man Albert would become, looking very much like his father as he stood up for what was right in the same calm manner. And yes, she got a glimpse of the rock star there too.

They held each other's eyes for a long moment. Albert looked like he was going to say something, but in the end he just nodded and waved.

Janna waved back. She turned to Eugenie.

"You'd better disappear."

"I could come with you," Eugenie suggested. "Maybe help . . . somehow?"

"No, I'll do this on my own. I'll meet you in my room later." With that, Janna squared her shoulders and went to meet her mother.

"Where have you been?" Carol asked as she got out of the car. Janna examined her, and yes, her mother looked a little tense.

"With Albert, um, working on a project. How was *your* day?" Janna winced. She couldn't have sounded more lame if she had tried.

But Carol had turned back into the car and was gathering her purse and a shopping bag. When she turned back, she looked as if she didn't know how to answer her daughter's question. For a few seconds Janna thought her mother was going to cry—she had seen Carol cry only a few times before, and it was never over something trivial.

But Carol's expression relaxed and she slumped against the car. Looking up, she stared at the stars. "My day was unbelievable."

Janna realized her mother had no idea of the things that Janna would believe now.

"Tell me about it," Janna said.

"Right after lunch one of Pizer's goons came and escorted me to Pizer's office, where I've never been in all the years I've worked there. I could hardly get the guy to say anything, his face was so carved from stone, let alone tell me what the meeting was about. So I tried to figure out what I've worked on lately that has gone either really well or really badly, but I couldn't come up with anything.

"When I got there, I realized that Pizer had finally figured out who I am. He cleared his throat and started this long drawn-out speech that sounded awfully like I was going to get downsized—that's their expensive word for 'fired'—but then the phone rang and it was his daughter, whom I've heard doesn't get along with him too well and apparently never calls, and Pizer shooed me away. I was almost out the door when he called me back. He was talking on the phone and scribbling something. Then he stood up and handed me a check made out to the school district. A rather . . . large check."

"You didn't get fired?"

"I've never been fired before, Janna, but I don't think that's quite how it's done."

"What did you do then?"

"I told him I didn't understand, and he said that he didn't either but he really needed to talk to his daughter now, and thanks for stopping by."

"And the school vote?"

"That's the other unbelievable part. The budget passed, and not by just a few votes either. Albertoo really must have gotten to people last night. People were positively *jolly* when I was at the polls."

They walked inside the house, and Janna felt some of the tension in her spine begin to fade. She let out an enormous sigh.

"And your day?" Carol asked. "That must have been some project you and Albert were working on. You look beat. What was it?"

"Sort of a combination humanities-economics project," Janna said.

Her mother handed her the shopping bag. "It's been such a weird day I almost forgot. I bought this for you at lunch."

Janna opened the bag to find a copy of *The Secret Princess*. She looked at her mother.

"I know what you did with your money, Janna, and I know how much you wanted to read that book. I don't want you to think that being kind means having to do without. I was very proud of you for giving up that book."

Janna leaned over and hugged her surprised mother very tightly.

"I'm a really lucky kid, Mom," Janna said. "And I know it."

Chapter 19

From her bedroom window Janna could see the Newbys' living room, where Mr. and Mrs. Newby were dancing slowly to the strains of something romantic. She sighed. It had been a glorious night, a night beyond her craziest fantasies, a night like no other. She felt like one of the Medieval Maids herself.

"So miracles really do happen," Janna said to Eugenie.

"This is better than a miracle—it's real," Eugenie said. "We just gave things a nudge and people kept passing it on."

"You didn't think it would work," Janna said.

Eugenie shrugged. "I've seen a lot of human behavior in my time. I've never seen anything quite like this."

"What will happen next?"

"I don't know. Every day everybody has the power to pass it on, or to stop it dead."

"I'll try to keep doing my part," Janna said.

Eugenie reached out and tapped Janna's knuckles with her own.

"I know you will."

Eugenie stood up and put on her purple coat and black galoshes. "And now I must be going."

"But I thought you were staying until warmer weather. Remember your wish? You can stay even though I don't have any genie watts left. We'll come up with something to tell my mom."

"Thank you, dear, but then I was afraid of not finding people kind enough to keep me warm and safe. I'm not afraid anymore."

"Where will you go now?"

"Out there." Eugenie waved toward the window. "Some other town, maybe some other country. A genie's work is never done. And I must say, you have somewhat restored my faith in your pathetic race. Now that I know what can be done, I'll not let my future masters waste a single watt on frivolous things."

"Take care of yourself," Janna said. "Stay warm."

"I'm thinking tropical. Someplace with real cabana boys. My patootie is so cold it has permanent freezer burn." Eugenie leaned in and hugged Janna tightly.

"Good-bye," Eugenie said. And then she was gone, bag and all. Lying on the floor where Eugenie had been was the purple hat. Janna picked it up and smoothed it out.

"Thank you," Janna whispered. She was still holding the hat when she heard her mother call from downstairs:

"Janna, why are you using your old coat?"